Praise for Lisa Girolami's Novels

Love on Location is "an explosive and romantic story set in the world of movies."—*Diva Direct*

In *Run to Me* "Girolami has given us an entertaining story that makes us think—about relationships, about running away, and about what we want to run to in our lives."—*Just About Write*

By the Author

Love on Location

Run to Me

The Pleasure Set

THE PLEASURE SET

by
Lisa Girolami

2010

ISBN 10: 1-60282-144-5
ISBN 13: 978-1-60282-144-6

This Trade Paperback Original Is Published By
Bold Strokes Books, Inc.
P.O. Box 249
Valley Falls, NY 12185

First Edition: April 2010

CREDITS
Editors: Shelley Thrasher and Stacia Seaman
Production Design: Stacia Seaman
Cover Design By Sheri (graphicartist2020@hotmail.com)
Printed in Canada

Acknowledgments

Many thanks to Tony, Sandy, Jeanine, and Karen for the banking information and much-valued help.

For the French lesson from Mary M, *merci beaucoup*.

To the crew at BSB—led by Rad, steered by Jennifer, guided by Shelley, Cindy, and Stacia, and "covered" by Sheri— I tender my deepest appreciation.

For Miss Willis, my eighth-grade English teacher, who believed in me and didn't mind that I was "different."

And to all the wonderful readers who turn these pages, I extend many heartfelt thanks.

Dedication

For Susan. My love, my laughter, and my protector.

PROLOGUE

She stood at the railing of a beautiful teak-and-stainless-steel backyard deck overlooking the expensive Hollywood Hills homes below. Night had fallen over the city long before, but she was not focused on the twinkling lights. She swayed as she attempted to stand upright, but she was clearly drugged and crying. Though mascara ran down her cheeks, she was luminously gorgeous, in the way those who lived the Hollywood lifestyle tenaciously pursued their movie-star good looks. The multimillion-dollar residence behind her was the kind most tourists only glimpsed as they drove down Sunset Boulevard below, craning their necks upward, wondering which actor, rock star, or movie mogul lived in this or that mansion.

A road leaving the residence wrapped around the right side of the house, then descended quickly as it curved around the back of the house, much farther below, around the fabulous deck, and continued down the hill, where it quickly disappeared. The perfect-half-circle road hugged the house from upper right to lower left, its curve only one of the many hairpin turns that pointed the way home and back for Hollywood's rich and entitled.

The house and street, like the majority of those up in the hills, basked in warm, subdued lighting, for those who could afford to live this high up preferred unhindered views without bright street lamps as much as they craved privacy.

The woman staggered away from the railing and stumbled back toward the house. Wide-open, oversized sliding-glass doors ran one-quarter the length of the house. Expensive burgundy curtains, of some imported lavish French textile, swayed lazily in the night breezes, licking the outside edges of the sliding-glass doors like furtive, sinewy arms seductively beckoning the woman inside.

She walked in and disappeared behind the opulent curtains into the architectural marvel.

A gunshot cracked, a macabre staccato of pop, pop, pop that reverberated, bouncing sickly back and forth between the hills. A dog barked, roused suddenly into the role of sentry.

Barely audible voices from other houses farther down the hill echoed as well. "What was that?" "Call nine-one-one!"

A few minutes later, a red Mercedes-Benz appeared from the right, at the top of the curved road, driving down toward the left, around the hairpin turn, not too quickly, not too slowly. It rolled farther down the curve and out of view.

More minutes passed and silence once more enveloped the hills. The street was dark and shadowy again. The dog stopped barking. Though a few lights shone in the house with the teak-and-stainless-steel deck, nothing moved.

A police car appeared, creeping up the road. It cruised up around the curve, toward the front of the house.

The police car disappeared around the upper right. Knocking sounded from the front of the house but went unanswered. A few beats later, two police officers walked down the right side of the house, along the deck that jutted out over the steep, sloping yard. They climbed over the railing and eased toward the open sliding-glass doors.

Suddenly, the one who had ventured closest to the doors jerked his head toward his partner. "A body!"

He pulled his gun, as did the other officer. They ducked down, covering themselves as the second one snatched his radio and called for backup.

As faint sirens called in the distance, both policemen entered the house through the sliding-glass door, guns drawn.

CHAPTER ONE

*W*hy *do beginnings have to be so hard?*
    Laney DeGraff gazed out the window of her Hollywood Hills home. It was early morning but the neighborhood was awake, with joggers, dog walkers, and one or two work-bound people backing their cars out of their driveways.

In the reflection she cast in her own window, she studied a snapshot of her life. At present, she was thirty-four years old. Her shoulder-length blond hair could use a trim, but maybe she'd let it grow as a symbol of some forthcoming inner growth. How would that ever happen, though, with the rut she'd been in for years?

She sighed and turned away from the window to inspect the recent indentations in the living-room carpet. The empty areas where pieces of furniture used to stand were ghostly reminders of their presence. Half the bookcase was bare, and a couple of pictures had been taken off the wall, leaving only the hangers embedded in the plaster.

Laney picked up her coffee mug and briefcase. Dressed in a blue serge suit over a tailored, white cotton blouse, and with a cell-phone earpiece lodged in her ear, she tuned back in to the conversation she was having. "Where will it be today?"

"Patina?"

"We had lunch there Monday, Hillary."

"My best friend is in crisis and I want nothing but the best. Again."

"You mean you want nothing but their best salad caprese."

"That too."

Laney paused, feeling as deflated as she knew she must look. "She's gone, Hillary, and as much as it hurts that it's over, this really pisses me off."

"Laney, you had a right to kick Judith out. She was cheating. You stood by when she started the Internet affair, hoping she'd stop even though I told you she wouldn't. It wasn't until she really stepped out and screwed you that you finally did what you needed to."

"I know, but God, it still hurts."

"Yes, sweetie, I understand. Meet me at noon."

Just after seven, Laney parked on the side of the First Bank of Rodeo, chirped her remote, and turned the corner onto the sidewalk. Every day she appreciated the luck that the bank enjoyed being situated amidst Cartier, Chanel, and Tiffany. She strolled past men and women dressed like executives, and others who looked more like movie stars and rock stars in their torn jeans and Von Dutch T-shirts, and entered the bank.

Laney visually inspected the sleek tellers who greeted customers and the account executives who were helping others. She barely noticed the grand mission style of the interior, long aware that its nod to classic architecture subtly proclaimed its solid dependability. Laney's father had chosen the style when she was a baby, and its symbolism still held true.

As Laney walked toward the back of the bank she greeted three or four customers with morning pleasantries and waved to another customer as she approached her office. "Bill, how's it going coaching those twins of yours?"

"Keeps me off the streets Wednesday nights!" The man turned from his teller and waved good-bye before he headed toward the door.

An attractive woman stood by her longtime secretary Kelly's desk.

"This is Theresa Aguilar," Kelly said, with her usual efficiency. "She's here to open a safety-deposit box and wants to speak with you personally."

Laney's office occupied a large portion of the bank's back

corner. Accompanying the woman to a leather chair, Laney greeted her with an open hand. The tall woman who grasped her hand firmly wore expensive Prada clothing and had a large matching satchel elegantly draped over her shoulder. Her uniformly tanned golden skin probably came from some South American ancestry instead of the sun. And Laney knew if she touched the woman's thick black hair, she would feel soft, luscious curls. Her eyes were so big and brown that Laney couldn't tell where her irises ended and her pupils began. And her lips had the sexy fullness Laney always equated with gorgeous Latin women. The woman was stunning.

Offering the woman a seat, Laney moved to her place behind the desk. "Ms. Aguilar, it's a pleasure to meet you. I'm Laney DeGraff."

"My pleasure, as well."

"I haven't seen you in the bank before."

"I opened an account the other day."

"Well, I apologize for not introducing myself then. I like to get to know all the customers personally, and I'm very glad you chose us."

"Do you know every customer's name?"

Laney paused, then realized that the woman had obviously noticed her talking to the customers as she walked through the bank. "I try." Laney offered her a business card.

"DeGraff. You're Dutch?"

"One half. The Dutch translation of bank president is 'she who must learn everything by rote.'"

Theresa smiled. "One half and what else?"

"German and English," Laney answered automatically, amused that the conversation had turned friendly so quickly. Silence stretched between them as they regarded each other. Laney smiled for no other reason than she was caught off guard.

"So you would like to open a safety-deposit box, Ms. Aguilar."

"Yes, I would. And it's Theresa."

Laney retrieved a form from her desk, although the account managers at the bank entrance usually handled those functions.

But many of those who patronized Rodeo Drive preferred, if not expected, the highest authority to handle their service.

"Would you like to list someone as an emergency contact for this box?"

"Do you mean if I die?"

"Or become incapacitated."

Theresa smiled. "No, thank you."

"Fine. Please fill out this form with your name, occupation, address, and other info here and sign here. Then we'll go to the vault."

When they reached the safety-deposit boxes, Laney said, "It takes two keys to open the box. The account managers have access to this pass key. Any time you need to retrieve your box, just sign in at the main desk and someone will help you."

Laney stopped at a row toward the back of the vault. "Here it is…number ten thirty-three. If you'll just insert your key here…" Laney aimed her key for one of the locks and, as she did, Theresa raised her key to insert hers. Their hands bumped together, and both women produced the uncomfortable smile of strangers drawn close.

"Pardon."

"Sorry."

After they unlocked the box, Laney pulled it out, and Theresa followed her from the vault and into the safety-deposit room. "Spend whatever time you need in here and just press this button when you're finished. I'll come back and return your box to the vault with you."

Before Laney could leave, Theresa pulled wads of banded cash out of her satchel.

"Wait, ah…hold on. I'm not supposed to be here when you do that."

Theresa looked at the money. "Oh, I'm sorry."

"No, I'm sorry. I didn't explain that we shouldn't be in here with bank customers. Your safety-deposit-box contents are confidential. And…ah…money. Legally we're not allowed to let you keep cash in the box unless the bills are out of circulation. Like for numismatics. Ah…currency collectors."

"Do you get a lot of those?" Theresa was smiling rather rascally.

"Yes, actually."

"If the content is supposed to be confidential, how would you know?"

Laney chuckled. "Good question. We wouldn't. But the paperwork you signed states the rule about money."

Theresa placed her hand on Laney's, which surprised her.

"Listen, Ms. DeGraff—"

"Laney." She allowed herself the pleasure of this woman's hand upon hers, glad she hadn't removed it yet.

"Laney, things are not good. My husband is cheating on me and I know he's planning to divorce me."

"I'm so sorry."

"I've become aware that he plans to take everything we have. I'm just trying to protect myself. He's a ruthless, powerful stockbroker, and his lawyers are even more powerful. They'll trace bank accounts, IRAs. This is the only way he won't be able to find this money."

Laney focused on Theresa's warm hand on hers. Reminding herself that it belonged to a customer, she directed her thoughts to the form Theresa had filled out. "Aren't you an attorney as well?"

Theresa laughed and slowly removed her hand. "Yes. But my specialty is criminal defense. My lawyers are good as well, but my husband has always been a dirty fighter."

Laney nodded. "I kicked out my partner of four years just two weeks ago." Why had she just revealed that fact?

"I'm sorry, as well. It's got to be tough."

"Kicking her out wasn't half as tough as finding the e-mails she'd been writing to someone in Santa Monica."

"Explicit?"

"Very."

"Jesus, that's painful." Theresa was now studying her with

a frankness that made Laney feel suddenly exposed. "You're too beautiful and, I'm finding out, too kind, to have that happen to you. Let her go."

"She does seem remorseful. Does that count?"

"Reread the e-mails you found and then answer that question."

Laney laughed. "Good advice. Thanks."

Laney looked at the money Theresa clutched in her hand and then into Theresa's eyes. Their gaze held steady for a moment. Finally Laney pointed to the cash and said, "I didn't see that."

As she turned to leave she wondered about Theresa's smile. It spoke volumes, the details of which Laney didn't quite understand. "Buzz me when you're done."

❖

Detective Sandrine Girard rocked back and forth in her squeaky office chair. The grating, high-pitched whine descended in tone as she leaned back and ascended as she tilted up. As much as she needed to get the chair fixed, the squeaking seemed to help her focus.

She reread the report she was about to give the chief of police. The recent fraud investigation she'd been assigned was wrapped up, with three suspects locked securely in jail awaiting their little chat with the judge.

When she had first responded to a phone call from the Beverly Hills branch of Security Fund and Loan, they gave her information about fraudulent accounts opened in their California, Nevada, and New Mexico branches. The crooks had stolen more than $50,000. The case had taken a lucky turn when one bank employee protected an area of her teller's window that contained a latent fingerprint from one of the suspects who had just come in to try to cash a check. Investigators from the Crime Scene Unit lifted the perpetrator's oily calling card and were able to locate him on their AFIS database. A few more days of research led to the identities of his two accomplices, and they were quickly picked up without incident.

She put the report down and picked up a piece of paper with a phone number scratched onto it. Though it had been about business, it was the first note Laney DeGraff had ever left her.

Laney DeGraff, she thought as she rocked back and forth. Even though this would be strictly a business call, she smiled.

"Girard, I swear I'm going to throw that chair of yours into the Dumpster outside." Detective Bruce MacRae had poked his head inside her door. He was in Homicide, which was right across the hall from Fraud. "Why do you insist on letting it squeak like that?"

Sandrine looked up and smiled unenthusiastically. "It helps me think."

"Let's try to think more quietly, huh?"

"You Homicide dicks are a tense bunch. Always concerned about every little thing."

"At least we don't have to worry about getting paper cuts from analyzing bad checks."

She liked Bruce. He was a police officer through and through and held his professionalism in as high a regard as she did. She often talked to him when one of them was waiting for a phone call or taking a break from the chaos. They badgered each other with friendly taunts and regularly shared the details of their personal lives. Best of all, he was one of the few detectives who didn't call her Frenchy or tease her about her accent. She could trust him, and that realization gave her a glimmer of hope that one day she could become whole.

"Are you handling the Hollywood Hills murder?" Sandrine had seen the crime scene photos lying on Bruce's desk when she returned a hole punch she had borrowed from him.

"Yeah. Beautiful actress type found dead in a gorgeous house on a private winding street way the hell above the cloud line. Who can afford those places anyway?"

"We'll never know."

"Seemingly great life. Quiet neighborhood. No evidence of a break-in."

"Husband?"

"Wasn't married. No boyfriend we've found either."

"Drugs?"

"She was high, that's for sure. She'd been crying, too. Maybe for her life. I don't know."

Sandrine started to rock again and Bruce frowned at her. Sandrine grinned. "How's the wife?"

"Good. How have you been? Still dating the tall one?"

Sandrine nodded. "Nothing to write home about."

A phone rang across the hall. "That's me," Bruce said as he threw a paperclip at her. "Quit squeaking."

She continued rocking until her last comment came back to her. She stopped rocking. *Nothing to write home about.*

Truly, she didn't have much to tell her father back home in Giverny, France. Felicia, the woman she had recently begun dating, wouldn't be the topic of any conversation with him. As much as Sandrine enjoyed her, nothing had sparked between them yet. She doubted it ever would. While things were pleasant, no embers of desire smoldered in her chest.

She sighed, feeling the full weight of her breasts as they rose and fell, then picked up the recent fraud report. All the loose ends had been tied up and she was even grateful that they had resolved it so quickly, so what was bothering her?

Leafing through the report, she was slowly turning the pages, seeing only black ink shapes on white paper, when it occurred to her that she was revisiting a persistent but futile notion. Why did she always return to the fantasy that she could ask Laney DeGraff out when the woman was clearly not available?

❖

Laney walked Theresa to the bank's main entrance.

Theresa paused. "What? No toaster?"

Laney chuckled, then shook Theresa's hand. "I'm sorry for what's happened at home."

"You're very kind, thank you. And you, too. Think seriously before you consider letting her back."

They both paused. Laney didn't know why she was drawn to this woman. Maybe because she had talked only to her best friend and Kelly about the breakup, and now this stranger seemed to be reaching out to her.

After Laney thanked her for her business, Theresa withdrew car keys from her purse. "Laney, I'm meeting some of my girlfriends at the Equinox later. Would you like to join us?"

Laney opened her mouth but wasn't sure how to respond.

"We meet because we're all in the same situation as you. Breaking up, broken up. It's sort of like a support group. With limos." Laney laughed comfortably as Theresa's hand went up in the air.

"We're not only the coffee-and-cigarettes-bitch-about-men types. We also band together to launch new business ventures, and I can assure you, they're lucrative. We help each other and make our own success happen, and best of all, we call the shots. Plus, I think you and I could be great friends."

Laney felt compelled yet hesitant to go. She had experienced an instant camaraderie with Theresa. However, she hardly knew her. Obviously Theresa lived a much more lavish lifestyle than Laney, but the draw between them was powerful.

Theresa appeared attractive and self-assured, and as Laney began to murmur, "I suppose—" Theresa immediately said, "The Equinox. Nine thirty," and gave her an address on Sunset and Vine. "Give them my name."

Before Theresa came into the bank, Laney had barely felt like getting to work and managing lunch with Hillary. Her breakup had sucked all the wind out of her. Though Theresa and her unexpected invitation had interested Laney, what she needed to do was go home after work, take a bath, wrap herself in a thick robe, and stare at the TV until sleep engulfed her.

❖

"Go." Hillary was sharing an appetizer of edamame with Laney at Patina. Hillary was Laney's age and they looked almost like sisters, though Hillary dressed as a young, full-time mother, not a businesswoman, like Laney.

"Why would I want to sit around with a bunch of women and listen to them bitch about their husbands?" Laney hadn't expected Hillary to encourage her to go to the Equinox tonight.

"Because it'll be good to bitch along with the rest of them."

"You don't bitch about Cheryl."

"Miles difference. Cheryl's an angel of a partner and doesn't fool around on me."

Laney nodded. "There is that quality, yes."

"More to the point, business deals can come from those kinds of bull sessions. Plus, it'll be good to express your anger at Judith."

"I am angry, you know that."

"But you haven't shown it. You're too friggin' nice all the time, Laney. She really mistreated you and you took it. And by the time you found all those e-mails to that other woman, they'd been at it for months."

"The irony, huh?"

"You bet!" Hillary almost cackled. "Throughout your whole relationship you said sex was almost nonexistent. Then when you did have it, she was pure vanilla."

"I didn't say pure vanilla."

"I'm summarizing. The point is, Laney, you had a boring sex life, and then all of a sudden, she's slamming another woman."

"For a mother of my beautiful little godchild, you sure are crude."

"Blame my five brothers. Listen, she abused your trust, she abused your kindness, and she abused your body by not using it. Sexually, I mean."

"I know what you mean." Laney blew out a long breath. "I've never really had a relationship where the sex was, you know, great. So I can't say she withheld passionate sex from me."

Hillary leaned closer. "Laney, I know you never felt passion for Judith. But even just regular sex or making love wasn't part of your relationship. Not for four years, as you yourself said."

"She never even tried. She was always too busy or too tired."

"You're too darn cute to put up with someone who doesn't want you in every way. And now we know that she used you, because it obviously wasn't about her not liking sex."

Laney grimaced. "I don't want to think about it."

"Well, it happened and you need to shout about it. Or at the very least, forget about her and go have a blast. Go out with your new friend. She's inviting you to the Equinox, for Pete's sake! You know you can't just walk in there. You have to know someone."

"Yeah, I think it's one of those underground Hollywood places."

"It is. And it's so exclusive, you become automatically cool just stepping past the threshold."

When the server brought their salads, Hillary slapped Laney on the top of her hand. "So go for me and then tell me all the details!"

CHAPTER TWO

What am I doing here?
Laney had debated whether to go out. Surely, a little time away from the disruption of what used to be her comfortable home would be a good thing. She didn't relish staring at the evidence of her absent relationship, because that would only remind her, for the thousandth time, how angry she was at her ex.

Why was she questioning an invitation to meet a straight woman at the hippest club in Hollywood? Because she usually didn't accept them from straight women? Because lately she had felt frumpy and unattractive? Yes. And yes.

Certainly she'd accepted offers of nights out with many business acquaintances in the past. Her position as president of the family bank necessitated that she build those relationships. Money, her father had told her, doesn't just walk in the door without some cultivating.

So why the big deal?

But as she reached the nondescript door of the address Theresa had given her, on a rather seedy side street off the famous corner of Sunset Boulevard and Vine Street, she finally admitted to herself the obvious if not absurd reason she was about to walk inside.

Theresa Aguilar was very attractive.

❖

Elegant 1960s music suffused the Equinox as Laney gave her name to the maitre d'. While he checked a leather-bound notebook,

Laney looked around. The interior ambience was nothing like the rough exterior. She had seemingly climbed into a time-travel machine and landed squarely in the suave year of 1968. Retro modern furniture and décor infused the place with a hip vibe, and chic people densely populated it.

Theresa was sitting in a room at the back of the club with about ten beautiful women. Their couches and plump armchairs formed a circle around a kidney-shaped retro coffee table that held drinks of all shapes, sizes, and colors.

Theresa waved her over, whispered briefly into the ear of the woman next to her, and when the woman got up to leave, Theresa took Laney's hand, pulling her down onto the couch in the newly vacated spot.

"Laney. I'm glad you came."

"Thanks for inviting me." Laney felt like a kid who had just been accepted into the secret tree house.

"Kay," Theresa leaned toward the woman sitting on the other side of Laney, "this is Laney DeGraff."

Kay had movie-star good looks, which Laney realized was appropriate because Kay was actually Kay Kitterman, the movie star.

"Hi, Laney."

"Pleasure," Laney said, a little starstruck.

"Theresa told us your girlfriend left you. I'm so sorry, honey."

"Actually, I kicked her out."

"Good for you." Kay leaned her head back on the couch, obviously comfortable. "*My* stinking-ass boyfriend decided to shack up with his leading lady while he's shooting his current movie."

"You mean Rance Edwards?" Laney couldn't believe she was conversing with a movie star. Sure, she'd seen many while living in L.A. and even spoken to a few that banked with her, but Kay Kitterman was a huge star.

"The very one. I'm sure it'll be in *People* magazine by Friday."

"Ouch."

"Yeah, it sucks."

Kay nudged Laney's shoulder with her own. "May I buy you a drink?"

"Tonight I get that pleasure, Kay." Theresa had placed a hand lightly on Laney's knee.

After they ordered, Theresa nodded toward nothing in particular. "This is called the back room. It's reserved exclusively for people who don't want other people to pay attention to them—actors, studio executives, producers, and their husbands, wives, boyfriends, whatever. That woman in the slinky black dress is Morgan Donnelly. She's married to the head of Kingdom Crossing Studios. I'm sure she's going on and on about her husband being a pompous prick."

"That's Morgan Donnelly?" Morgan bought and sold many businesses in Beverly Hills and Hollywood and was considered one of the big shakers and movers in town, but Laney had never seen a picture of her.

"Yes, it sure is. Her husband separated from her a few months ago, but he's probably regretting it now that she's hired the best attorneys in L.A. He'd be better off to stay married to her and continue his affairs on the side. Lord knows, she does."

"Theresa." A woman came up behind Theresa and placed a hand on her shoulder.

Theresa turned. "Laney DeGraff, this is Candace Dooring."

Laney recognized the famous TV actress right away. She was a well-covered celebrity and often appeared on entertainment shows and in magazines.

"Hello, Laney." Candace squeezed her hand.

"Hi."

"How are things?" Candace said to Theresa, and right away Laney picked up how stiff they were toward each other and how obviously they lacked warmth.

"Well, Candace. Very well. I owe you a lunch."

She turned to Laney. "How do you know each other?"

"We met at my bank. Theresa opened an account there."

Candace's eyes darted to Theresa and then back to Laney. "That's good to hear." She smiled at Laney and added, "And you're as cute as a bug's ear."

Theresa's laugh didn't sound sincere. "I'll call you about that lunch."

"Very nice to meet you, Laney. I'm sure I'll see you again." Candace nodded curtly, then blended into the crowd behind Laney.

"Don't worry about her, she's not a happy person lately."

"Why not?"

"No good reason."

For a while, they fell into casual conversation. A few women interrupted them to say hello to Theresa and chat briefly. When Theresa leaned away to speak with another woman, Laney stopped to take stock of her circumstances. She was definitely out of her league.

Sure, she was the president of a bank on Rodeo Drive in Beverly Hills, but truth be known, the bank was one of the smallest in town. Though Laney was used to wealthy customers, she had never really rubbed social elbows with any. Certainly, business functions kept her in the network of the elite, but none wanted to simply hang out with her like Theresa did.

What could she offer these high-powered women? She hadn't married into money and didn't have servants at home or pictures of herself in magazines. She downed her second drink a little too quickly and coughed.

As if Theresa could read Laney's mind, she reached behind her and took Laney's hand in a reassuring grasp.

Theresa turned back around to face Laney. "Nervous?"

"What? No. Well, a little."

"Why?"

Laney jiggled her empty glass, wishing it would refill itself again. "This is all so exclusive. I'm a working stiff who doesn't go out to private clubs."

"Don't give me that blue-collar shit. You're the president of a bank."

"It's a small family-owned bank. I draw a good salary, but the rest goes back into the business. Rather blue-collar."

"We're not that different, then. Customers aside, this business is rather blue-collar."

"This place?" Laney was confused.

"The Equinox. It's a business that has to be run like anything else. Employees, inventory, taxes."

"You own this place?"

"Well, we girls do." Theresa made a circling movement with her head to indicate the women sitting around her. "It's a hush-hush kind of thing. None of our husbands or boyfriends know because we engage in financial opportunities of our own, without anyone else controlling or manipulating us. We simply like to run things our way and turn a profit on the side."

Laney knew her mouth had dropped open, but she was truly amazed. "You said opportunities. There are others?"

"Yes. It's quite a little racket." Theresa laughed.

"After I work hard all day at the bank, I usually go straight home. That's about all I have in me most days. And after a long day as an attorney, you have the energy for this. That's amazing."

"None of us does this alone. We help each other in our businesses. Combined, we have the acumen and experience to make things happen."

"And you do so in a fantastic club that you own. Now that's what I call a clever enterprise."

"It is, but these women are no more or no less normal than anyone else walking down the street. Everyone goes home alone sometimes. Right now, we're a group of women who have difficulties in our relationships. Some choose to stay in them and be lonely, and others get dumped on their ass. But everyone needs support. We just also happen to make money on the side."

"I'd like to be part of that, Theresa."

"I hope you do. There are a lot of opportunities out there. We formed this group so we could take control of our lives. Together we're powerful, and we have a hell of a good time."

"I feel a little guilty having so much fun while making new business connections."

"Guilt tastes bitter, Laney." Theresa raised her glass to Laney's and clinked it solidly. "To you and me and our new partnership, whatever that will be. And as far as anyone not liking the way we live our lives, fuck 'em."

As they talked and laughed, Laney realized she hadn't thought about Judith in several hours. She was surrounded by women who encouraged each other and promoted confidence. She relaxed on the couch a while longer, watching the next part of the evening pass in a montage of curious impressions. The women all seemed very close, and because Laney was intrigued she simply absorbed things as they happened.

Theresa threw an arm around her at one point, immersing her in an intense conversation, their faces just inches apart, a lot closer than she was used to. Another woman sat on Theresa's lap as she introduced herself to Laney and explained that her boyfriend was out of the country on a philanthropic trip. Again. Two other women huddled in a seemingly deep conversation periodically punctuated with loudly clinking glasses. And the few other women that were too far away to talk to gazed at her with what looked like smiles of approval.

Clearly these women were all moneyed or positioned well in Hollywood, but they seemed extra close. Maybe it was akin to the Hollywood kisses everyone gave each other in this town. Chic pecks between business associates and friends or even distant friends were a common practice. And while the responsible part of Laney tried to convince her to take the opportunity to do some bank networking, she was enjoying herself too much to disturb the evening's vibe.

Sometime after midnight, Laney told Theresa she had to get home so she could be at the bank the next day at her usual time, seven a.m.

Theresa walked her outside the Equinox, where a crowd of paparazzi jumped into action, snapping pictures of them. Some knew Theresa's name and asked about her husband.

"Theresa, does being a lawyer make it hard to be married to a stockbroker who has been in criminal trouble in the past?"

"Is it true you're planning to represent Steven Shaffer, one of the biggest criminal minds in Los Angeles?"

"Your husband is being investigated by the SEC. Any comments?"

"Theresa! Who's that with you?"

Theresa hugged Laney and whispered in her ear, "Get used to this. You're in with us now."

As the cameras clicked away and voices called out for their attention, Theresa tightened her hug, holding Laney longer than she had expected her to.

"Sleep tight," Theresa said.

As Theresa made her way back into the Equinox, Laney started for her car. A few of the paparazzi followed her, trying to get her to speak to them, but Laney kept her head down, ignoring the noises behind her.

When she climbed into her Mercedes, she let out a huge breath. Having so much attention was electrifying but also a little intimidating. She was finally able to pull away and, just as quickly, the paparazzi turned back toward the Equinox.

❖

"Kay Kitterman?" Hillary had stopped eating when Laney finished giving her the details of her evening at the Equinox. They sat at a small table outside Café Erewhon, under the shade of a *Tipuana tipu* tree. Laney had just come from the bank and was dressed like any other female executive in Los Angeles, while Hillary wore stylish sweatpants and a workout top.

"Crazy, huh? And Morgan Donnelly was there. She's married to the head of Kingdom Crossing Studios."

"Hollywood's biggest business tycoon?"

"None other. Hillary, it was like a who's who of power women. And doctors, attorneys, authors. Oh, and Candace Dooring."

"You're kidding. I watch *Cyber High* all the time."

"She's on that show, too?"

"You need to turn on the TV every once in a while." Hillary laughed. "Well, my best friend has just entered the inner sanctum of Hollywood's elite."

"One night of drinks hardly counts." But Laney was still bubbling over.

"It sounds exciting, anyway."

"It was great. I felt like a celebrity. I mean, you read about all that Hollywood glitz, but when you're in the middle of it, it's tremendous. The paparazzi actually swarmed us when we left. They were after Theresa, not me, of course, but it was a real high anyway."

"Wow. So you're gonna end up in *People* magazine now, huh?"

"I doubt it. Anyway, the women I met last night were really nice and supportive."

"The underground parties and glamorous settings don't hurt either."

Laney agreed. It was a bit self-indulgent to imagine becoming a full-fledged member of such an elite group, but the possibility thrilled her.

"So how was Theresa?"

"Fine. She's married to a guy named Roger Aguilar—some powerful Wall Street trader or something."

"Is she really attractive and Latin American looking? I remember seeing a magazine picture of this gorgeous woman and some Wall Street bigwig."

"That's probably her. And the bigwig is screwing around on her with some woman who's also a trader."

"That's terrible. And divorce isn't an option?"

"Seems messier than that. She's afraid he'll take everything and leave her with nothing. So she's trying to keep the façade going a while longer while she protects herself financially."

"She's gotta be pretty angry inside."

"I suppose. But we sure had fun last night. She was a blast!"

Hillary watched her a moment. "Last night was good for you, huh?"

"Made me forget about Judith."

"Has she gotten her stuff out of your place?"

"Three days ago."

"Good riddance, then."

Laney attempted a smile, but it felt more like a pained grimace.

"And hey!" Hillary used her salad fork for emphasis. "It sounds like you have a new pack to run around with."

"Sure wish you could hang out with me."

"Cheryl and the baby are all the pack this dog can handle, thank you. Isabelle's second birthday is coming up this Sunday. Will you be at the party?"

"I wouldn't miss my godchild's party for anything."

CHAPTER THREE

Sandrine sat in her unmarked police-issue car under a sweeping oak tree in the Griffith Observatory parking lot. She sobbed as she gripped the steering wheel, unable to stop the tears that flooded from the deepest, scariest place in her heart. She had awoken at five a.m. from a reoccurring nightmare and been unable to shake its horror all day. Finally at lunch she escaped the claustrophobic confines of the police department and barely made it to the observatory before the racking tears blurred her vision and body shakes kept her from steering safely.

The nightmare was the same as usual. She was six years old and standing in the kitchen with her mother. The cupboards and refrigerator were empty and she was starving. She was too terrified to ask her mother for food, but she'd die if she didn't. When she finally whispered the words, her mother said, "I'll feed you when I get back. Trust me, Sandrine."

Driven by her aching gut and the lie she knew her mother was telling, she said, "But you never do."

Suddenly her mother smacked her mouth and then shoved her to the floor. Too scared to look up, Sandrine listened to her mother rush out the door. As her mother walked away, she spoke in a voice that seemed three octaves lower than usual. "Trust me, Sandrine," she said, then cackled. The words and cruel laughter slashed through Sandrine's physical pain and made her cry in anguish.

She stared out into the forest surrounding the observatory. After Sandrine had suffered years of emotional and physical abuse, strategically delivered when her father wasn't around, her mother finally abandoned them both. Her father never left her side after that, but he also never knew about the abuse until much later. When Sandrine was a child, she was too ashamed to tell him. Worse, she never told him that she believed her mother left because she had been bad.

Her father was her savior, reading her French fairy tales until she fell asleep each night and cooking wonderful meals for her, so she always knew she would never be homeless or hungry. But the words "trust me" haunted her solitary childhood so completely that she couldn't trust anyone but her father.

Though her mother was, at times, stable enough to perform minimal mothering tasks, the intermittent, unpredictable cruelty had destroyed Sandrine's ability to believe that everything was okay, even when things were calm around the house. And though Sandrine now realized it wasn't her fault that her mother left, she was still convinced of one thing: trust was an illusion.

Although she trusted her father, her inability to trust others had not only stunted most of her relationships but caused other problems in her life.

A car pulled into the parking lot. Thankfully, she had already stopped crying. She took a deep breath, wiped her face with her shirt sleeve, and turned on the car's ignition.

Get back to work where you belong.

❖

The First Bank of Rodeo was unusually busy for a late Thursday afternoon. Laney's phone hadn't stopped ringing and her ear had stayed plastered to it.

"I'll send the branch expansion plan in an e-mail, Kent. Yeah, it's a pretty tight plan. I asked David to look it over as well so the next step is to put an estimated budget to it. Yes. Maybe two weeks…"

The intercom line was blinking. She looked up at Kelly, whom she could see just outside her office. The windowed top half of the office's front wall gave her a view of Kelly and most of the bank when the privacy blinds were open. Kelly had her ear to her receiver and waved at Laney.

"Kent, I've gotta run. I'll get that e-mail to you within the hour." She punched the intercom line.

"Your father's coming by."

"Thanks, Kelly."

A half hour later, Edgar DeGraff walked into the office. Though it had been five years since he retired and turned over the presidency to her, he never left the house without being immaculately groomed and attired in one of his handsome Armani suits.

"Dad."

"Good afternoon, Laney."

He handed her some paperwork and sat down in one of the chairs facing her desk. "Thank you for e-mailing me this retail business development report. I know you don't have to check in with me anymore, but I appreciate it."

Laney waited for him to continue. He didn't stop by unless something was really good or really bad.

"Retail accounts are up thirty-one percent over last year. That's amazing. You've done an incredible job, Laney."

Laney smiled. "We said we'd go after them hard."

"You went after them hard."

"There's a team behind this, Dad."

"Yes, there is. And that's why I made the trip out here to thank the leader."

"Thank you."

"I suppose I should be thanking *you* for accepting the president's position. It's an arduous job, I know. And you're doing well."

After they talked a while longer, he rounded the desk and kissed her cheek. Laney watched him walk out and stop at Kelly's desk to shake her hand. Though she couldn't quite hear his words, it was clear he was catching up with Kelly's life, as he always did when he stopped by. The phone rang and Kelly glanced at Laney, clearly not wanting to interrupt Laney's father.

She held up a hand, motioning to Kelly that she'd get the phone herself. "Laney DeGraff."

"Laney, it's Theresa."

"Hello! How are you?"

"Doing great. Did you get home okay?"

"Yeah. The cameramen left me alone as soon as I walked toward my car. You?"

"Just came from a steam and a massage. The last of my Patrón Platinum molecules are floating around in eucalyptus vapor back in Westwood. I wish you could have joined me."

Tequila that cost two hundred and fifty dollars a bottle wasn't usually a weeknight splurge for Laney. Actually, it was never a splurge for her. "Sounds like fun."

"There's nothing like feeling the steam roll over your naked body. You'd have loved it."

"Thank you for last night. It really helped me get out of my head. I've spent the last couple of weeks with my face hidden in a stack of books."

"No place for a magnificent woman like you, Laney."

"Self-imposed incarceration is the martyr's playground."

"You shouldn't choose to be a martyr, darling."

"What fun would that be?" Laney liked the light discussion, which was odd because the conversation with this straight woman bordered on playful teasing.

"I can't imagine that hiding in your bed reading books is fun for you."

"Maybe my morals demanded that I lament my breakup for a while."

"So you let life control what you believe is right or wrong conduct?"

Laney admitted that she did sound pretty pathetic. "I guess I need to look at my morals a little closer."

"You can start with this very one."

"So what should I learn from this new enlightenment?"

"Isn't it obvious?"

Laney thought about her recent solitary nights. "Don't be a hermit?"

"The lesson is a little more positive and pleasurable than that, Laney."

"Let your hair down and party like a rock star?"

"That's more like it. If you give me your address, I'll pick you up at nine."

Another night out? And on a Thursday night? If she and Judith went out at all, it was either on Friday or Saturday, never both nights, and especially never during the week. And they always came home early and went right to sleep. No romance, no sex, usually not even any kissing. And of course toward the end, they never went out on weeknights because Judith always went out to do "extra work" in the evenings, after coming home briefly from her office job.

"I've got a pen and paper."

❖

Theresa's black BMW moved smoothly down Santa Monica Boulevard, eastward past Highland Avenue. The area was just east of the more glamorous Beverly Hills and West Hollywood areas and in the middle of the "working man's" Hollywood, which was where all the companies that supported filmmaking were located. Film-editing and equipment-rental companies supplied their services to the studios and independent film producers in seldom-remodeled 1930s- and 1940s-era structures. In between those businesses sat dilapidated buildings with crumbling sidewalks populated by homeless people and a smattering of rent boys and girls.

"Where are we going?" Laney breathed in the crisp, pungent smell of the new leather seats.

"A meeting place where we hang out. We're a block away."

"Interesting choice of neighborhoods," Laney said, and Theresa nodded, obviously expecting that response.

"This is one of the places we go where there are no cameras or nosey people. It's our little hideaway."

They pulled up to an old storefront with a rusting sign that read Manny's Tire Store. The neighborhood was definitely unsafe, especially at night, for two women parking a rather expensive BMW at the curb. Laney looked around uncomfortably for anyone who might pose a threat.

Instead of entering the building via the litter-strewn front door, Theresa guided Laney to a side door that a passerby would scarcely look at twice. The broken streetlight made it even scarier.

Because the Equinox had turned out to be a surprise, given its underground location and ramshackle exterior appearance, Laney went along with this adventure as well. Theresa must know what she was doing.

After they walked through the first room, Theresa gave Laney a tour.

"Gracie, who was at the Equinox with us last night, is an interior decorator. I let her loose and she had her way with this place. She turned this old tire-repair waiting room into our lounge."

Sure enough, what had probably been folding chairs, cheap coffee tables, and single-bulb light fixtures had been replaced with lush plum-purple silk couches, mahogany-and-glass tables, and posh pendant lighting. The walls were painted a surprising, but strangely complementary, burgundy with little gold fleurs-de-lis.

Though devoid of people, the room had a well-appointed audio system that played velvety jazz.

Theresa took her to another room, where Kay Kitterman and five of the women from the Equinox were mixing drinks at a grand bar, stocked with every type of alcohol imaginable.

"This was the old back office. It took Gracie forever to get rid of the smell of sweaty men, but as usual, she did an expert job. We call this the Queen's Salon."

And, fittingly, the room was designed in a style that must have been inspired by the 1940s *Queen Mary* luxury liner.

Opulent dark wood wainscot walls and ostentatious ruby carpet set the stage for oversized caramel leather chairs and small, round gold-leaf drink tables. Period chandeliers glistened in the low light, and the only item out of place was a very large plasma TV screen.

Kay stood and hugged Laney. "You made it!"

Theresa and Laney settled on a sumptuous sofa and someone brought them drinks.

"What is this?" Laney sniffed the russet-colored drink.

"Cinnamon rum cures. Very trendy. You'll like it."

It was good. The spicy concoction warmed her throat as she took small sips.

"So," Theresa said, "what did you say when Judith asked you to get back together?"

"She hasn't."

Theresa nodded. "She will."

"I broke up with her and made her move her things out. I told her we were finished."

Theresa looked intently at her long enough that Laney began to fidget. "What?"

"You may have told her you were through with her, but I'm not sure she was convinced."

"Why do you say that?"

"I can read your face. You're not a hundred percent convinced right now that she needs to be out of your life."

"She needs to be gone. I don't care what she says or does."

"Mark my words, she'll tell you she fucked up and she still loves you and can't you forget the whole mess so you can get back to your lives."

"Do I look like a pushover?"

Theresa smiled. "Not only do I get paid to read the body language of my clients, but that of my adversaries and their clients as well. I can even read the judges. As hurt as you were, I'm sure you didn't want to break up in the first place, but her cheating forced you. So I bet she saw a little uncertainty in your expression. She'll ask you back. Just be ready."

Two women sat down together on a large chaise lounge. They giggled for a moment, then kissed, their lips lingering longer than was customary for friends or even for the typical Hollywood kiss.

Theresa said casually, "They obviously have a crush on each other."

As the music played well into the night, the gathering took on more of a party feel. Eventually, the conversations gave way to random pairs of women dancing in the middle of the room.

Theresa and Laney talked about Laney's work and Theresa's law practice.

Finally at one a.m., Laney told Theresa she had to go.

"Stay a while longer, Laney. The night has just begun. Have another drink and I'll drive you home soon," Theresa said as she got up to go to the bar.

Laney had deliberately stopped drinking an hour earlier so she could fall right into bed and get a good night's sleep.

Morgan Donnelly and Candace Dooring plopped down on the sofa.

"Laney, how are you?" Candace asked.

"I'm fine, thank you."

Candace bumped her knee into Laney's. "Are you married?"

"No. I just broke up with my girlfriend."

"Oh. I hate breakups. I had enough of them before I married my husband. It's so much easier now. I mean, we have a nice life together and we do what we want. There's no drama as long as he gets to have the fun he wants and I get to do the same."

Theresa had been talking with some other people but returned to sit on the sofa arm next to Laney. "Morgan owns an art gallery on Melrose. We rolled some of our investments toward the start-up money for it, and now she's doing incredibly well."

"That's fantastic," Laney said.

"It keeps me off the street." Morgan smiled. "Well, sometimes."

"I really should get going," Laney began, but stopped when Theresa bent down and whispered, close to her ear, "I have some questions about valuation discounted cash flows, and you're the perfect person to answer them. Stay just a little longer."

Laney felt a light kiss on her ear, then a warm breath caress the side of her neck. She raised her eyebrows in surprise. This was certainly an interesting group and by far the most thrilling experience she had been part of in a long time. These confident, beautiful women had taken her into one of the most exclusive private groups in Hollywood. They were powerful and assertive. The mix intoxicated her.

Leaving now was like turning down dinner with Angelina Jolie. She didn't want to send the message that she wasn't interested in this opportunity. Another hour wouldn't hurt.

❖

When Laney got home Judith was waiting on the front steps.

Laney bristled at the surprise visit. "It's a little late, isn't it?"

"I came to pick up the last of my clothes."

Laney stood there, contemplating what to do, then waved her head toward the inside of the house.

Judith walked in and headed for the bedroom.

"They're not in the bedroom, Judith."

She turned, looking pained and hurt.

"Dining room."

She disappeared into the dining room and reappeared with two black garbage bags of clothes. She walked toward Laney, who still stood at the door, hand on the doorknob. When she got a foot or two from Laney, she stopped. They stood there in silence for a moment.

Judith sighed heavily. "I screwed up, Laney."

Laney didn't respond.

"I've been doing a lot of thinking. I mean, four years together. It's been a great relationship. I made a huge mistake. And I went to get counseling. I'm seeing a therapist twice a week. I wanted to tell you that I'm taking full responsibility for what I did. I won't say that I was bored or that you changed and that's why it happened. It was me. I screwed up."

Judith's face shifted to something that looked like sincerity, and Laney began to falter inside. She bit her lip to keep from saying anything that might show that she wished things hadn't gone so badly. Laney knew Judith wanted some feedback, but she remained wary of what she might say and held out until Judith continued.

"I had broken it off with her long before you saw those e-mails.

I mean, you saw for yourself that the e-mails stopped weeks before. And when you and I split, I fell into a depression. Then…then I kicked myself in the ass and realized that you and I were meant to be together. I've recently been spending my nights either working or going to therapy or just journaling about my feelings for you. About us."

The more Laney heard, the more a rumbling pain welled up inside. She had been so dedicated to Judith, even when Judith started to pull away emotionally. And then she was not only gone, but in the arms of another woman. And now this regret from her? What else would Judith say?

"Don't get mad, but I called Hillary. She gave me hell, I'll tell you! Ripped me a new one. I told her that I still love you and that I'm working my ass off in therapy. I'm so sorry to have put you through this. Can we please start over?"

Laney processed all this surprising information. She had been cast aside, forced to send Judith packing while never really wanting to. But Judith had made her decisions and had flouted their agreement to be monogamous.

"Laney, say something. Can we give it another try?"

The anger that burned in the bottom of Laney's stomach replaced her uncertainty. "She said you'd do this."

"Do what? Who?"

"Come back with this bullshit."

"Bullshit? I *love* you!"

"She said you'd say that, too."

"Who the hell are you talking about? Was it the woman who dropped you off?"

"A friend, that's all. A friend who's been there."

"Who? Some friend you're sleeping with?"

Laney's fury swelled, spreading up her body. Now was the time to break free from the unhealthy patterns of her past. Her ears grew hot and she took a deep breath. "I am done being a victim, Judith. I was crushed when your affair broke us up, but I've moved on."

Judith lowered her head and shook it. "I'm sorry, Laney. I screwed up. I want to make this work." She looked up. "Please, can we get back to the relationship we had before? I know I shut you down emotionally. But I know how to fix that now."

How Laney had wanted to hear those words many months ago. Before the Internet called Judith away. So many nights she would have taken Judith's offer. That's all she had ever wanted.

Obviously it had taken the shock of losing her to make Judith shape up. Laney knew she'd never let Judith dupe her again, but was that enough?

"No, Judith." Laney was on overload. She had too much to think about. "This is too difficult."

"Please just consider it. I want to have dinner with you tomorrow or the next day and explain some things. Just give me that, for now."

CHAPTER FOUR

Laney knew it was late and probably impolite, but she had to talk to someone. She hated to call Hillary because, with the baby, they were most certainly already asleep. When Theresa answered on the second ring, Laney felt suddenly calmer.

Theresa was right, Laney's head kept repeating, she knew this would happen. "Theresa?"

"Laney? What's the matter?"

Hearing Theresa's poised voice made her feel remarkably watched over. "It's Judith, my ex."

"What happened?"

"We had a fight."

"Don't move. I'm coming over."

"You don't have to—"

"I'm in West Hollywood, give me twenty minutes."

When Theresa walked into Laney's house she took her confidently by the hand and led her to the couch. "Okay. Spill."

Laney recounted the conversation and added that she had acquiesced to Judith's appeal for dinner.

"I mostly just wanted the conversation to end. To get her out of the house. I don't know what else I need to hear from her."

"Probably nothing, Laney. What does your gut say?"

"I don't know. I'm pretty confused. Mostly I'm mad at myself for allowing her to take advantage of me for so long and then betray me like that."

"Picture her back in your house. Living with you. Tell me now what your gut says."

"She'd be in the guest bedroom, that's for sure. And she'd be skulking around trying to get out of the trouble she caused." Laney shook her head. "That would make me pissed off and miserable. I wouldn't like feeling that way at all."

"Then go have dinner with her and keep that in mind."

"Shouldn't I cancel dinner?"

"It's up to you, darling. But remember, it's not a one-way talk. It would also be your chance to tell her the things you didn't say tonight. And I'm sure, as you work this over in your head between now and when you see her next, you'll come up with a lot of things. Use dinner to get them off your chest." Theresa smiled and opened her arms. "Come here."

Laney fell against her.

"I know she hurt you terribly, Laney. And I know how that feels. She started this, but you can end it by telling her it's truly over. You'll find the strength. Don't worry."

As Laney lay in Theresa's arms, the smell of spicy perfume enlivened her. Judith always wore flowery fragrances, but the days of those sickly sweet smells lingering in her bathroom were over.

❖

Sunday crawled by and Laney hadn't done a damn thing that was remotely productive. She had gone out to the Tire Store again the night before and gotten quite drunk. Theresa wasn't there, which disappointed her, but she spent the evening with Kay, Morgan, Candace, and six other women. She remembered dancing passionately and laughing wildly and finally crawling into bed at six a.m. The whole day passed with a loathsome groggy sensation she hadn't subjected herself to in a long time. She gave in to a long nap on the couch, and while she felt a little guilty about the unattended laundry and dangerously empty refrigerator, it had felt luxurious. All day long, however, Laney wavered between wanting to go to dinner with Judith and wanting to call off the whole thing. But if she canceled dinner, Judith would find another way to approach her.

And Theresa had told Laney that going would give her the opportunity to get all the hurt and anger off her chest, which she really needed to do. Then she could truly end it.

❖

Laney and Judith were an hour into their dinner, their meals having just been cleared off the table, and so far Judith hadn't said anything different than she had the night she'd come over.

Laney had listened to various versions of "I'm sorry" and "I screwed up" and "Please take me back" but nothing that explained why Judith had been so closed off most of the relationship or why she had been unfaithful.

The more Laney heard, the angrier she became. It was too little, way too late. Finally, she took her turn. She'd never liked confrontations but had a lot to say about four years of being in an unsatisfying union that ended with an insensitive betrayal. And as she formed her words, she imagined how the self-assured Theresa would respond and knew what she needed to say.

"Judith, I don't care anymore about how crappy you feel. And I don't care anymore about what you want." *And I'm sick of feeling vulnerable.*

Judith's eyes opened wide. Rarely was Judith at a loss for words, but Laney's newfound strength had stopped her dead. Emboldened by this reaction, Laney continued. "You treated me badly, then fucked me over. It's done. It's over. I'm not interested in taking you back. You blew my trust in you and that's that."

"Well, this is nice, isn't it?" Judith seemed to recoup quickly from her shock. "Courteous, quiet little Laney is now shoving it up my ass. I came here to tell you that we all make mistakes. I made a big one but I want to try to work this out."

Laney knew she had unleashed a firestorm even bigger than the harsh encounters she and Judith had in the painful days before they broke up. But she was pissed. It was time to conquer her old wait-because-it-will-get-better idiocy and face reality. She would never be the Laney she had been in that relationship. And it became amusingly apparent that someone else had also just changed. The nice version of Judith had disappeared.

"And now you're acting so high and mighty," Judith said, "that you can't see you're throwing away four years together."

"Correction." Laney could have been channeling Theresa. "You threw the relationship away. You walked all over me before that, shutting me out, getting angry and nasty when I tried to talk to you, then finally fucking around. I'm glad you had this nice dinner, Judith, but here's something else to swallow. You're out of my life." *And I refuse to let anything like that ever happen to me again.*

"Wow." Judith suddenly appeared eerily calm. "I see your new friends have helped you with this little script, huh?"

"What the hell are you talking about?"

"Theresa, the lawyer, and all her Hollywood celeb buddies."

"How do you know about her?"

"It's not hard to know about her. I recognized her face when she dropped you off that night and finally placed it. Everyone knows that she's a royal bitch. So now you're in the Pleasure Set with her. And them."

"The Pleasure Set?" Laney hadn't been aware that the group actually had a name. "They don't call themselves that."

"No, you're right. That's what everyone else in Hollywood calls them."

"I'm sorry, I couldn't hear you. Could you spit out your words just a little nastier, please?"

"They're a bunch of prima donnas who hang out in a secret club and act so exclusive that they have to raise the doorways so they can get their upturned noses in. They're all about drinking expensive champagne, throwing money around to buy this and that, and not caring in the slightest what anyone else wants or needs. They're just an elite bunch of rich women who feel exceedingly entitled and cherish getting their pictures in magazines. Great goal you achieved there, Laney."

"Why should I care what you think?"

"Sure, why should you care? Because you've turned into a fucking bitch, too, that's why. And it's obvious all you care about is yourself. Jesus, Laney! You missed your godchild's birthday party."

Oh, shit. Laney had forgotten about the party earlier that day. She had wasted the entire day recovering from her all-nighter. Hillary would be so disappointed. And rightly so. Laney felt awful.

"You've got your head up your ass, Laney. What's gotten into you?"

"Judith, I really don't need to sit here and have you berate me. What I do with my life now is none of your business."

"What happened to the nice Laney I knew?"

"You mean what happened to the nice Laney who just shut up all the time and went along with whatever you wanted? She got cured, thanks to you." The words came out sharply but she felt surprisingly good.

Judith bristled and clenched her napkin. "I'm glad I found out about this side of you. Christ, I can't stand to look at you anymore."

Most of Judith's reaction obviously came from Laney's abrupt shutdown, something she had never done. And the venom Judith spat out just then was truly uncalled for. What she did now was definitely none of Judith's business.

Laney stood up to leave. "Go fuck yourself."

CHAPTER FIVE

Laney pulled herself into work quite late Monday morning. She was extremely tired from the weekend, and the bitter taste from her dinner with Judith still sat stale in her mouth. She'd called Hillary to apologize for missing Isabelle's birthday, which had been so abnormal. But lately things hadn't been normal. Hillary was, without a doubt, disappointed. Laney told her she'd make it up to Isabelle by taking her out for ice cream soon.

Kelly called her on the intercom. "Laney, Detective Sandrine Girard is here to see you."

For the last few years, Detective Girard had handled all criminal issues related to Laney's bank. Their paths crossed when there was evidence of stolen checks, fraud, credit card scams, or any of the other creative ways that people tried to make someone else's money their own. Laney always called her when she noticed any of her bank customers behaving suspiciously, but she hadn't seen the detective in four or five months.

"Good morning, Detective." Laney invited her to sit down and realized that she was even happier than usual to see her.

"Good morning. And when do you plan to call me Sandrine?"

"I suppose it's about time." Detective Sandrine was always very nice and extremely professional. And unlike Judith, Sandrine looked Laney directly in the eyes when she talked to her and paused to contemplate what she had just said before responding. Of course, Sandrine was there on business, and her job required that she listen intently, but Laney was rather sure Sandrine also conducted herself like this even outside of work. It was a very attractive trait.

"How are things in your life?"

They had had enough casual conversations to discover that they were both gay. "Going fairly well."

Sandrine tilted her head slightly. "The picture of your partner is gone."

"We broke up."

"I'm really sorry."

"Well, at first, I was, too. But it's definitely for the better."

"Then I'm glad to hear that."

Laney smiled. She'd always had a good rapport with Sandrine. The tall, attractive woman had short, thick black hair and glowing green eyes. Her French accent had seemed to mellow in the years she'd spent on the Beverly Hills police force.

"Thank you for coming by so quickly."

"Would it be unprofessional of me to say that I always put your messages at the top of my list?"

"Not in the least." Was Sandrine being friendlier than normal? Maybe it was because Laney was now no longer coupled and unavailable. Or maybe Sandrine was always this forthcoming but Laney hadn't allowed herself to notice before. "I also have to admit that I've made my customers wait sometimes when I knew you were on your way over."

"Well, crime has to be dealt with promptly." Sandrine grinned. "If that's what you meant."

"Not really."

"In that case, you made my day."

Laney handed her some paperwork. "This is the information we gathered about the check kiting we uncovered. They deposited a bum check into the first account number that I've written down there."

Laney had seen check kiting in her bank before. Usually it was easy to detect. But because it typically involved depositing and drawing checks at two or more banks while taking advantage of the time it took for the second bank to collect funds from the first bank, the funds and the criminals were usually difficult to catch.

"And I assume that before you could verify that the check was unfunded, they wrote a check against that account."

"Yes. Within twenty minutes. But here's the strange part. Rather than move the money to an account at another bank, someone else wrote a check against that same account. And guess what? They came in here to cash it."

"Well, it sure makes it easier when they actually appear in the bank to withdraw the cash." Sandrine glanced at the paperwork. "Are they both on the tape?"

"Yes. Plain as day."

"Have you seen them before?"

"No."

Sandrine smiled kindheartedly and Laney smiled back. It was a little silly, but Laney felt safe around her. The detective regarded her intently and Laney grew warm inside. She took Sandrine to the back foyer where the security equipment was housed. Tapes were stacked on top of a metal box, one pile marked "Ready" and the other pile, "Recorded." She reached to the side of the piles and pulled out a lone tape.

"Here it is. As you must know, we insert a tape every day and keep two weeks' worth, rotating them as we go. I had this one marked and the record tabs punched out so it wouldn't get recorded over."

Sandrine was standing very close behind her. Laney had always considered Sandrine lovely, even fascinating. Now that she was single, she found being this close to Sandrine incredible. Her immediate proximity ignited a heat inside Laney, and a sudden desire flashed inside her. Her thighs twitched and she gulped down a breath. It would have been easy and natural to melt back into her, and Laney wanted to do just that. She closed her eyes, trying to quell these unprofessional feelings.

What was going on? Had she suddenly unleashed her wanton libido onto the world? First Theresa had appeared in her life, and now Sandrine was standing right behind her, stealing any proper sense she had.

Sandrine was here on business. And this was a public bank. For those reasons, and, admittedly, to buy herself a little time to allow her logic to return from its sudden departure, Laney had to restrain the feelings that had just flared up inside her. Instead of following her desire, she moved forward a little, then turned around to face Sandrine. That way, maybe her obvious longing wouldn't be in extreme close-up.

Sandrine stood there with a roguish expression. Laney was convinced Sandrine had read her body language correctly. But all Sandrine said was, "Let's take a look at this tape, then."

❖

As Sandrine drove away from the police station parking lot just before six that night, she pondered why she had been in such a great mood all day. Granted, it was heart-rending to hear that Laney had ended her relationship with Judith. Breakups could be very difficult.

Even though Laney had said it was for the better, she knew Laney's heart had been hurt and she felt for her.

Guiltily, she also felt hopeful about the change in Laney's status. She had had a huge crush on Laney since the day they met. She had often thought about Laney and had carried quite a torch for her. Of course, it became apparent right away that Laney was in a relationship, but secretly, Sandrine often wondered what it would be like to have Laney's heart. Sandrine's previous lovers had all been dark with brown eyes, and she wasn't sure why. But Laney certainly was not that type. Sandrine liked the golden blond hair that rested gently on Laney's shoulders. And Sandrine had always been enthralled with Laney's eyes, the color of tumbled blue sea glass. She imagined Laney to be a romantic lover and considerate partner, based on the way she interacted with her customers and employees.

Sandrine's recent dating history had not been satisfying. She hadn't clicked with anyone on all levels. The women she dated were either beautiful but empty, or nice but too unlike her in personality to make a decent match. And the few relationships she had been in were disappointing.

She had never been able to trust her lovers. Sadly, she understood the connection between the trauma of her mother's abuse and the way she now distrusted people. The one person she needed to rely on to care for her, love her, and never leave her had abused her, seemed to hate her, and eventually abandoned her. A seed of despair had been growing in Sandrine's soul since then—the knowledge that she had developed the ability to pick women who lied and misled her. Her first couple of lovers had crushed her heart like her mother had. And though she hadn't given up trying, she hadn't found anyone who could challenge her conviction.

The woman she was currently dating was nice enough, but like it had been with all the others, Sandrine couldn't ease up on the gut feeling that made her suspicious of the woman's intent. She and Felicia had been seeing each other for about a month. Felicia had deep mahogany skin and eyes and was tall, with broad shoulders and wide, sexy hips. As a real-estate broker, she was very motivated and full of energy, and Sandrine liked the time they spent together. They hadn't slept together yet, but they might.

So would that change now that Laney was single? Sandrine had a fairly practical view of dating. It didn't necessarily mean with only one person at a time, which was probably the best way to sort things out, but, with limitations, dating more than one person could also work. She just didn't like the possible drama. Clear lines of communication were always crucial. Nevertheless, things could get sticky.

Felicia was open to dating others while they were going out, and they had agreed to tell each other if they had slept with, or were planning to sleep with, someone else.

Quickly Sandrine's thoughts returned to Laney. A bolt of excitement raced through her as she pictured Laney at the bank just hours earlier.

When Laney took her to the security equipment, she could

have sworn Laney was attracted to her. Once, Laney froze, seemingly disconnected from the business at hand and tuned in to Sandrine's presence right behind her. Sandrine believed that desire swept through Laney because of the way she stood there, breathing deeply, seeming almost afraid to turn around. And when she did, her beautiful features were flushed with something that looked like longing.

Sandrine wanted to kiss her right then. Without a doubt, that would have been the wrong thing to do. She was there on business, but the desire had still gripped her.

She turned from Santa Monica Boulevard onto Laurel Avenue and drove the one block north toward her house, all the while hoping that Laney would go out with her but not wanting to push anything so soon after Judith's departure.

Sandrine didn't want to be a rebound. However, even if they did date, many of her own trust issues and fears would probably come up and she might bolt. And, given that possibility, she hesitated to start anything. But she so much wanted Laney to be the one she could finally depend on.

If Laney would accept a date, Sandrine would be as careful as possible. The chance to be with Laney was too wonderful and too important to screw up. But would her old demons return to obliterate any opportunity with her?

CHAPTER SIX

While the thought of a hot bath and early bedtime tempted Laney all day, she succumbed to Theresa's invitation to meet the girls at the Tire Store.

By eleven o'clock, she was with ten women in the Queen's Salon and five others were out in the customer lounge. Dance music pounded from the sound system, and the extraordinarily large plasma TV played a strange movie showing mostly nude women at a party in a lavish mansion. Some wore leather collars attached to leashes that other women held. They all had seductive smiles, and Laney couldn't keep her eyes off the screen as an orgy slowly began to unfold.

She was slouched down in a thick, comfy couch next to Kay Kitterman, who was stoned on something. Nudging Kay, Laney said, "Did you know we're called the Pleasure Set?"

"We're called a lot of things." Kay slurred her words, her eyes set in happy slits. "Bitches, nefarious nymphs, whores." Her voice trailed off to a murmur.

"My ex used the term as if it were a terrible thing."

Kay shrugged. "I dunno. It's just a name. People are always jealous. We're in, they're out. Out, looking in."

Theresa wandered over and sat down on Laney's other side.

"Naked women floating on rafts in a pool with sushi on their stomachs," Laney said aloud. "And other women being pulled around by their collars. Doesn't this seem a bit depraved?"

Theresa sighed indifferently. "It's a Hollywood tradition."

"The Oscars, now that's a tradition. This one, I never knew about."

"It's a statement about the empowerment of women. When men make women wear collars or lie around naked, they're treating them like objects or whores, making them feel powerless. But look closely at these women. Do they seem powerless?"

Laney continued to watch the movie. It became apparent that the collar-bound women were managing themselves quite well.

Theresa's leg was pressed into Laney's, and with the movie she was watching, coupled with the heat of Theresa's thigh against hers, Laney's head swirled and she began to get aroused.

"In an S-and-M situation," Theresa continued, "who do you think is really in control?"

From her other side, Kay giggled and squirmed, but Laney was too absorbed in what she was seeing and hearing to care. "The dominated ones?"

"Yes. Those women have power," Theresa said. "Look at how they're controlling their activities. And another thing, they're more powerful than you or I as we sit here right now. We're hiding behind our clothes. They're standing there, lying there, saying, 'Fuck you for your shame, I'm not hiding. I'm wearing my power proudly.' Do you feel sorry for those women?"

Laney stared at the screen. One collared woman was on top of her leash-holder, grinding her pelvis in slow gyrations while the other looked up in yielding ecstasy. "No."

"They certainly command our attention, don't they, Laney?"

Laney nodded.

"Power and control. Like I said, it's a Hollywood tradition, honey. But not all power and control comes from men in suits."

❖

Tuesday and Wednesday were busy days at the bank, made more difficult because of Laney's recent late nights. She was out until four a.m. Monday night at the Tire Store, and then on Tuesday night, when Morgan Donnelly and some of the women took over the back room of the Equinox, they talked about new business ideas until the sun began to rise over the streets of Hollywood. Morgan had said Theresa was busy being a wife that night, but she and the rest made sure that Laney had an exceptionally productive time.

The prospect of becoming involved in some of their business ventures sounded very inviting. What Laney lacked in creative thinking, she could certainly make up for in financial expertise.

Quarterly bank financial reports were due, and Laney would be spending hours reviewing the details. She struggled through lunch, realizing, when her stomach rumbled, that it had been a week since she'd had lunch with Hillary. With the way her inbox was filling up, however, it might be another week before she saw clear to grab a bite with her best friend.

But she really wanted to talk to Hillary. Things were moving along with Theresa in a way Laney hadn't expected. She thought Theresa was hot and was definitely attracted to her, but she never imagined that Theresa might return the interest. Not that she had, exactly. But their conversation about the porn film Monday night hadn't felt like their usual run-of-the-mill chats. While Theresa hadn't touched her with more than a thigh against hers, Laney had become remarkably aroused.

Then again, after four years of living with Judith, a pedicure would arouse her.

They were growing close, but Laney couldn't tell if Theresa was just being friends or was interested in her.

Would she pursue a straight woman? She'd never considered it. Though Laney admitted that she was a bit sheltered, she knew those kinds of things happened. And people had sex without being in relationships all the time. The thought of sex with Theresa populated her thoughts. It had to be nothing short of amazing. Theresa was confident and strong and poised. And she was astonishing as well as commanding. Laney had never been with anyone like what she imagined Theresa to be—a sexual tiger that would take Laney and devour her for dinner.

Wait! Where the hell is this train of thought going? Theresa's married. Just calm the hell down and enjoy the new friends you're making.

Kelly broke into her fantasies. "Phone call on line two."

"Laney, it's Theresa."

The three words sent a buzz of excitement through Laney. "Theresa, hello." She hadn't expected the phone call.

"I will not take no for an answer. Be ready at ten tonight. I'm coming by to pick you up."

Laney laughed. "Where are we going?"

"It's not so much where we're going as what we'll be doing."

"So, what will we be doing?"

"Fucking the system."

Theresa hung up. Momentarily surprised and confused, Laney shook her head and said to herself, "I have absolutely no idea how to dress for fucking the system."

CHAPTER SEVEN

Mug shots of three Hondurans stared back at Sandrine. The two women scowled at the camera, and the man, looking more disheveled than the others, appeared uninterested.

So these were the bad guys who had tried to kite checks at Laney's bank. Sandrine was happy they had been able to identify these people. They had achieved justice swiftly, and she would be able to see Laney sooner to tell her of the outcome of the investigation.

Rocking back and forth in her squeaky chair, she wondered whether Laney would accept an invitation to dinner. She might, but Sandrine didn't want to appear pushy. However, it was just dinner, so hopefully Laney would say yes. The energy generated between them at the bank, even though unacknowledged, was palpable. Sandrine didn't think she misread anything, though Laney might not be interested in that way. Or she could already be dating someone else. Or others. She certainly was single now and unquestionably attractive.

But after a number of years of thinking about Laney and considering every time she visited the bank a high point of her day, Sandrine didn't want to miss an opportunity to get to know her better.

She hadn't been with anyone on a deep, serious level in two years. Her last relationship had been good for a while, but when her lover deceived her, too many painful memories of childhood emerged. All her dates since then had been pleasant but unfulfilling. Not a single woman had caused her heart to say yes.

Laney, however, was different because Sandrine had been able to spend a lot of time getting to know her without the possibility of dating her. She now considered her a great businesswoman and a kind friend.

Everything she knew about Laney encouraged Sandrine. It was time to exorcise the loathing she had suffered at the hands of her mother and the bad memories that haunted and manipulated her. If she pledged her heart to someone once more, especially if it could be Laney, she would go all the way.

She would call her tomorrow and ask her out. Hopefully she would say yes.

❖

The huge black Suburban drove down the Hollywood freeway with Laney and several other women from the Pleasure Set inside. It exited at Gower Boulevard, traveled south, and turned into Kingdom Crossing Studios.

The Suburban rolled up to the guard gate at the entrance. Laney and five others watched as Morgan waved some credentials out the window. Security promptly let them in.

They parked on the studio's back lot, by old Western movie sets and the southernmost soundstages, and piled out of the car. Theresa carried some manila envelopes while the rest carried bottles of Cristal and Dom Perignon, and Morgan led them into a darkened soundstage. As Morgan fumbled around with the huge door and a few women chuckled and giggled, Theresa rested her hand gently on Laney's shoulder. The door swung open suddenly and brilliant lights came on inside, revealing the elaborate sets of a motion picture obviously in production.

"What movie is this?" Laney asked.

Kay Kitterman led them toward the first set. "This is Rance's new motion picture. He's starring with that bitch he's fucking around with."

When they got to the set, Morgan switched two klieg lights on. Laney took in the room, which appeared to be part of a trendy New York apartment. A big picture window looked out onto a huge still photograph of the New York skyline.

As Theresa, Morgan, and Laney sat on the couch, the others pulled up chairs and they formed a small circle in the middle of the set.

Morgan drank from a bottle of Cristal. "Welcome, ladies, to our newest, if only temporary, office."

Kay guffawed. "May our success be better than Rance's. And I'm gonna dump his cheating ass after he wraps this movie."

Laney smiled and turned to Theresa to share in the amusement, but Theresa was frowning at Kay. What an odd reaction. Did Theresa disapprove of the breakup? Laney was about to ask when Morgan tapped Laney's knee with the bottle. Laney accepted it, took a long swig, and gave it back to Morgan. "So this is fucking the system?"

Theresa nodded. "It's doing whatever we can think of that's against the rules of those in power—our husbands, boyfriends, whomever. We're not supposed to be here but we make ourselves at home anyway. The system says you can't do this or that, and we say 'fuck you.'"

Morgan added, "Cindy Marrans took us to Universal Studios a few weeks ago. She's a studio executive there, and her husband is on the board of directors. In the middle of the night we snuck up to the *Psycho* house to smoke a little dope. The challenge was figuring out a way to get around security and not get caught."

"Why do you all do that?" Laney said.

Theresa answered as if it was obvious. "Because we can."

Kay laughed. "Another time Theresa got us into the L.A. Superior Court at night and we partied on the judge's stand."

"Aren't you all afraid of getting arrested or fired?"

"My husband may run this studio but he would never have me arrested." Morgan chuckled.

Theresa emitted a buoyant guffaw. "She has a tape of him and his lawyer discussing certain 'personal financial gains' at the expense of the studio."

"Isn't that a little risky?"

"Yes, but," Theresa casually took the Cristal from Laney, "it's a Hollywood tradition. Sometimes we party, but tonight, it's back to business."

Theresa opened the manila envelope and handed out some paperwork to each woman. "As you know, Morgan has opened her art gallery and the grand opening is coming up. Since we're investors in that effort, we can now parlay some of the profits from sales into a new venture.

"Take a look at the prospectus. PS Holdings has been set up to filter the profits into other lucrative opportunities that will yield returns we can draw from at our discretion."

Theresa turned to Laney and looked at her as she added, "Laney, we would like your bank to handle the transactions."

"That would be great," Laney said, excited that she was in on the ground floor with such dynamic women.

After they discussed the details of PS Holdings, they celebrated by passing around the libations.

At some point, Morgan got up to sit with Cindy on a chaise lounge, leaving Theresa and Laney alone on the couch. A while later, someone turned off one of the klieg lights, which threw Laney's half of the set into darkness.

With Theresa's arm around her, Laney felt the warm hand lightly rubbing her shoulder. She was a little buzzed from the champagne and let herself relax into Theresa's side.

Some of the women had disappeared into the darkness beyond the set, and soon the sweet, verdant smell of marijuana wafted toward her.

"I'm glad I could talk you into coming out with us tonight," Theresa said.

"This certainly beats a night in with the TV."

Laney watched as Morgan cuddled with Cindy. They were giggling and nuzzling each other's neck. Theresa traced a gentle line down Laney's cheek with her hand.

Laney was beginning to understand this group of women. Though most lived conventional lives, being married or having boyfriends, they all had one thing in common: they longed for excitement and diversion. And while Laney surmised that she might be the only true lesbian in the group, that didn't seem to matter. They had found camaraderie in this group, where they could get away from their conventional lives, pursue their own business prospects, and be whoever they wanted.

Enjoying the softness of Theresa's hand caressing her face, Laney let her head rest on the back of the couch and closed her eyes.

Some of her companions were obviously cheating on their husbands and boyfriends, but they were also being cheated on or, at the very least, ignored and unappreciated. Maybe some of them would be gay if things had been different. However, their lives had all taken a specific course and apparently they didn't want to change what they had built. To them it was better to maneuver things in a way that served their true desires. Regardless of their original decisions, why should they deny themselves a little pleasure?

Laney raised her head when Theresa's breath swept past her temple. And as Theresa delicately kissed her cheek, goose bumps rose on Laney's arms.

"Is this all right?" Theresa whispered.

Was it? Theresa was married. But her husband was a boor who was trying to pilfer all their money before he divorced her. Theresa had said he was cheating on her as well.

But all these facts vanished when Theresa began to rub Laney's stomach. In the back of her mind, she knew this was wrong, but she didn't care. "Yes," she answered.

Theresa slowly kissed her face, caressing Laney with her lips. Her hand continued to move across Laney's belly, gripping her at times when Theresa took a breath of excitement.

Laney turned her head to meet Theresa's lips, but Theresa wouldn't allow the kiss.

"Lay your head back again," Theresa said as she moved to Laney's neck, tenderly nipping her and heating up her skin with her breath.

Laney's head whirled in anticipation of more, craving Theresa's lips on her own. The exhilaration that Theresa's touch caused amazed Laney. No one had ever spent so much time on any one area of her body. Theresa's kisses on her neck and the hand that massaged her stomach were driving Laney out of her mind.

A hammer of lust pounded in her brain, causing a throbbing frenzy between her trembling legs. She wanted to push Theresa down on the couch to return the pleasure she was feeling, but that obviously wasn't what Theresa desired. And whatever Theresa wanted at that moment, Laney would absolutely allow.

Somewhere from the darkness, she heard movement, and the women who had wandered off returned to the set. Theresa's kisses slowed and she said, "We should go now."

Laney opened her eyes. She was breathing hard. *Ahhh! Don't stop!*

Theresa smiled affectionately and cupped her cheek. She stood and took Laney's hand to help her up. "You're amazing."

As they drove back in Morgan's Suburban, Laney sat in the backseat with Theresa on one side and Kay on the other. Her thighs still throbbed and she wasn't quite sure why Theresa had chosen that exact time to leave the soundstage.

"You do understand that we keep these evenings to ourselves," Theresa said.

Laney nodded.

"You're free to talk about whatever you please, but most of us aren't. And we don't want a lot of revealing talk."

"I know."

Theresa placed her hand on Laney's knee. "Are you okay with that?"

Laney smiled. Yes, she was.

CHAPTER EIGHT

Laney's nights out with Theresa and the other women were definitely not conducive to early morning productivity. Her mind had been scattered lately, and she was having a hard time concentrating on financials, deposit reports, and interest statements. She was contemplating her third cup of coffee when Sandrine called.

"I have some information for you on the kiting incident."

"That was quick." Laney's delight at hearing from Sandrine had nothing to do with resolving the case. Her exhilaration when they were in the foyer by the security equipment had been powerful. Sandrine, who was an attractive and charming detective, was now more than that. Laney was open to her feelings for Sandrine, and just hearing her voice drove that awareness home.

"Remember, you go to the top of my list."

"I do remember. As a matter of fact, that very flattering comment was hard to forget."

Why didn't she feel at least a little puzzled by this flirtation with Sandrine? After all, she and Theresa had also gotten closer the night before. Granted, Theresa had only kissed her neck, but obviously Theresa wanted more than just friendship. Then again, Sandrine made her feel so important. It wasn't the same kind of importance that Theresa's red-carpet life created. Sandrine made her feel important in a profoundly emotional way that stirred deeply within her. And even though they'd only spent a moment in back of the bank with the security tapes, the closeness of their bodies felt much more real.

"I'm very glad to hear that. And I'm happy to have caught you."

"Kelly will always put you through to me, guaranteed."

Sandrine chuckled. "That's great to know." She paused and then said, "After reviewing the tape you gave us, I can tell you that you were hit by a clumsy group of criminals."

"I suppose dim-witted thugs are a blessing?"

"My favorite kind. They were easy to identify on the surveillance tape. We were able to match them to other kiting scams in Santa Monica and Westwood and piece together their whereabouts."

"That's good news. Thank you, Sandrine."

"I'm delighted that we could resolve it so quickly."

There was silence on the other end of the phone line, and Laney wasn't sure if Sandrine had been interrupted by a colleague or was distracted by something else. Then Sandrine said, "Laney, would you like to have dinner with me Saturday?"

Laney was caught off guard. In the last week and a half, her life had been so different from the last four years. She had been out more nights than she ever remembered. She felt alive and excited.

She was free to pursue anything she wanted. She was single and could date other women. But focusing on Theresa, given her married status, wasn't necessarily the healthiest idea. Sandrine was single. And she came to the bank only when someone had perpetrated a crime, but her appearance had always brightened Laney's day. Each time, they conducted themselves professionally but took time to talk in depth about the world outside their careers, and Laney was always left with a feeling of excitement.

Once, when Laney's father was still working in the bank, he'd told her, when Sandrine had left after one of her visits, that it was obvious Laney fancied the detective. She had outwardly waved off the comment at the time but it stayed with her.

Laney knew Sandrine had been single more than she had been coupled over the past few years. And Laney had been with Judith. She had been devoted to her relationship so she'd never considered Sandrine as anything more. But now things were different.

A rush of exhilaration engulfed her. "I'd like that very much, Sandrine."

When she hung up, a huge smile erupted. *Sandrine Girard! Detective Sandrine Girard! Oh, my gosh!* She had never imagined she would be going on a date with Sandrine. She was incredible— intelligent and sexy and striking. And Sandrine's integrity was apparent in the way she carried herself.

I guess my father was right.

Giddy, she doubted she'd be able to work much after the phone call.

❖

It was Saturday morning and, except for some laundry and vacuuming, she had no plans. She lay in bed until almost ten, luxuriating in the fresh breeze blowing through her open windows.

She marveled that she could lie in bed all day and do nothing if she wanted. Usually, Judith was up at dawn planning some boring outing for them that made Laney dread getting up on her days off.

Had they really been boring outings, though? As she lay there reminiscing, she realized that the things they did weren't necessarily boring but that the connection between them had been virtually nonexistent.

They had had a proper relationship, filled with normal activities but without emotional closeness. Even boring activities would have been enjoyable if they had been able to respond to each other on a level deeper than light cheek kisses and assumed contentment. But as much as Laney tried to make the relationship deepen, she had failed. Still, she remained steadfast because she had made a commitment to Judith. And while finally breaking up with her was a hurtful relief, it was all the more painful to find out Judith had given the emotional relationship Laney truly desired to someone else.

Laney shook her head, annoyed. The missing sexual side of Judith didn't have any trouble appearing for what's-her-name.

But now Laney was energized with the possibilities of dating and even, did she dare to say it, stimulating sex. Admittedly, it was a bit superficial to focus on sex, but she had denied herself, or rather Judith had denied her, good, healthy sex for too many years.

Why shouldn't she look forward to some fun? She could do whatever she wanted to and whatever felt good. And Theresa definitely seemed to advocate that philosophy, even though Laney didn't sense that their connection would ever deepen beyond the physical.

As far as Sandrine was concerned, Laney wasn't sure where things might go with her, and it felt right to simply focus on dating and getting to know her. However, she couldn't help but steal moments from her day to imagine making love with Sandrine. The chemistry between them was unquestionable. But her mind also drifted back to non-sexual thoughts of Sandrine. She was a classy woman, and Laney wanted to get to know everything about her.

She blew out a full breath. *Slow down, girl.* Being suddenly single had caused new events to happen quickly. Dating meant going out with different people to see what she liked and didn't like. Theresa and Sandrine were light-years apart in personality, and why shouldn't she date around and see what she wanted? She had decided too quickly that she liked everything about Judith and look where that got her.

She didn't want to jump into another relationship that seemed one way but ended up another.

❖

Laney was halfway through a cup of coffee when her cell phone rang. Was the call from Hillary? Laney hadn't been in touch since she apologized for missing Isabelle's birthday.

As she brought the phone to her ear, she could hear background noise from a busy street. "Hello?"

"Laney! It's Kay. I'm on Melrose at a Starbucks. Get down here, we're going shopping."

Though she had spent time with Kay in group settings, this was the first time she had gotten a phone call from her. She assumed

Theresa had given her the number, and while one friend giving another friend her phone number wouldn't seem out of the ordinary, this friend was known to the whole world. And she was calling Laney to hang out.

She sat up in bed. "Starbucks?"

"Yeah. The one on Melrose between Curson and Stanley. Get your ass moving."

"Okay! Give me twenty minutes."

"Then I'll have time for one more triple espresso."

❖

Melrose Avenue was humming with the energy of a city that never slowed down. Cars crisscrossed the streets, people walked with full shopping bags, and diners ate and talked animatedly at outdoor tables.

Reporters doing stories about Melrose Avenue rarely failed to use the term *trendy* to describe it. Everyone knew that it was the gawk-when-you're-shopping and shop-to-be-gawked-at district. Hardly an issue of the popular entertainment magazines didn't contain at least a photo or two of celebrities glimpsed on the famous street.

They hadn't even reached the first store on their walk from Starbucks when a few paparazzi were already snapping Kay's photo. By the time they reached their fifth store, the group of photographers had grown to six.

"Doesn't all this attention get tiresome?" Laney asked when one of the store managers had to come out onto the sidewalk to escort them in.

Kay shrugged. "It's a Hollywood tradition."

Laney furrowed her brow. She'd heard that saying a lot lately.

Kay and Laney were now in Alexander McQueen, which was a first for Laney. She always avoided the store because its sleek, antiseptic white interior design and few, but extraordinary, clothing displays gave her the impression that the prices would be astronomical.

And she was right.

As Kay plucked three dresses from the racks, Laney contentedly followed her around, knowing that any credit card action in that place would come only from Kay's purse.

Kay handed her one of the dresses. "Here. We're trying these on."

Laney could have refused, but she was having such a fantastic time that she figured trying on the expensive dress didn't mean she'd be committed to purchasing it. But she soon regretted the decision. At a just-above-the-knee length, with a beautiful V-neck design, the black cocktail dress was exquisite.

"Oh, my God," Kay said when they came out of their dressing rooms to compare looks.

Laney took in the red and black evening dress Kay wore. "You look magnificent."

Kay waved her comment off. "Laney, look at this dress on you! How freakin' sexy are you?"

Laney turned to the mirror and Kay came up behind her, squeezing her shoulders. "Theresa's gotta see this!"

"Theresa?"

"She'll love it."

"Kay." Laney turned toward her. "I'm not going to buy this dress."

"Are you kidding me? It's sensational."

"It's also really expensive."

Kay made a short motorboat sound with her lips. "You're a bank president and you can't afford it?"

"Sure, I could afford it, but it's not practical."

"Since when is being practical a decree? Don't be a boring prude."

When Laney turned back to the mirror, she saw Kay's face just behind her, smiling devilishly.

No, I'm not boring. I might have been boring once, but not anymore.

"I'll take it."

CHAPTER NINE

Laney wore a comfortable but elegant pants outfit Saturday night. The weather was perfect and typical for Los Angeles, and the night temperature promised to hover around seventy-eight degrees. Sandrine picked her up and they made their seven-thirty reservation at Crustacean with ten minutes to spare. The restaurant's Euro-Vietnamese cuisine was always outstanding, and though Laney was looking forward to an evening of dining on royal tiger prawns, she was especially excited about spending time with Sandrine.

Her favorite detail about Crustacean was the famous walk-on-water entrance. A sub-floor, glass-covered aquarium ran like a calming river through the cocktail area and led diners to the main dining room. The remarkable interior design evoked a French Colonial estate like the restaurateurs' own home in Hanoi.

During appetizers of crispy satays and shrimp mousse, Laney sipped wine. "Tell me about your work."

"Other than visiting bank presidents? I keep busy with all different kinds of fraud cases. It may bore some people, but I enjoy piecing together the evidence and arresting those who believe they can steal others' hard-earned money."

"Well, I, for one, am appreciative."

"The bad guys never take a vacation in this town."

Laney laughed. "There are too many opportunities here."

"That there are."

Laney felt incredibly comfortable with Sandrine. The way

Sandrine's eyes sparkled when she spoke was wonderful, but what really warmed Laney's heart was the way they sparkled when she was listening. Sandrine's attentiveness made Laney feel heard and understood. "This may sound inappropriate, but I've thought about you over the years. You've always been so nice and easy to talk to. I never would have considered pursuing anyone while I was with Judith, but I always thought you were attractive."

"Not inappropriate at all, Laney. Just because you're in a relationship doesn't mean you don't notice other people. Of course, I'd never have pursued anything either, but I'm very glad we have the chance tonight."

"Me, too."

"Was your breakup difficult?"

"Yes. Judith had an affair and it took me a while to figure it out. I mean, I should have been more aware, but things change in a relationship. Sometimes people get a little complacent, but you're supposed to work through the slumps. I have to admit I hadn't been happy in a long while. Maybe she did me a favor by finally forcing the breakup. I might have simply remained there."

"Sometimes it's easier to stay where you are than take a step in a different direction."

"I suppose I was a little scared, too. Our relationship became a cocoon that I wrapped myself in. I let Judith make most of the decisions and just went along with things."

"Yet you were unhappy."

"Very." Laney looked down, swirling the wine in her glass. "We hardly talked about deeper things. The intimacy fell off." Laney inhaled deeply and blew out the air, remembering the discontent she had suffered. "Actually, it was never really there. At least not the way I wanted."

"That's an important part. Intimacy isn't just for the sake of pleasure. Our souls need to feel safe as well. It's essential in a loving relationship."

When Laney looked back up, Sandrine was smiling. Her face glowed with warmth, and Laney could have fallen into that tenderness.

"Where were you when I needed that exact advice?"

"I wish I could have been there. It hurts to know that you were deprived of a fundamental but vital part of who you are."

"Well, I can say that when it was finally over, I vowed never to let myself get in another situation like that."

"That's a good vow. Never deny your heart."

"Somehow," Laney believed her words with everything she had, "I don't think I ever will again."

Dinner came but Sandrine's eyes never looked away from Laney's. From her periphery, Laney knew hands were setting plates down and then they were gone. Delightfully delectable aromas wafted up from their plates but for a moment, nothing else was discernable.

Then Sandrine inhaled deeply and sighed. "Wow."

"Wow is right." To be enfolded in such concentrated attention felt divine and a little overwhelming.

"You are amazing, Laney."

"I…you…" Laney couldn't find words to go with her feelings.

"Those are good words to put together."

Laney couldn't agree more. She reached out for Sandrine's hand. "Yes. But the way you look at me takes all words away."

"Tu me rend tellement heureuse."

"What does that mean?"

"I'm sorry. I didn't mean to slip into French." Sandrine pursed her lips reverently. "Your words made me happy and that's what I just said."

Sandrine was so in the moment, with her attention, her focus, all for Laney. "My words made you happy? That's really nice. I like that."

Sandrine's gaze lingered. "Actually, the exact translation was, you make me so happy."

Something akin to a padded mallet seemed to strike Laney, sending her breathing into overdrive. Sandrine's allure was dazzling, but what she meant left her stunned.

"Your mouth is open," Sandrine said softly.

Laney blinked. "I was thinking about a movie."

"Which one?"

"Bell, Book and Candle."

"With James Stewart and Kim Novak. It's a lazy-Saturday-afternoon or staying-home-sick favorite of mine."

"You're like Kim Novak."

"A witch?"

Laney shook her head. "Bewitching. Enchanting. Captivating."

"I hope those are all positive aspects?"

"Better than that. You're definitely spellbinding."

"I'm flattered to be compared to Kim Novak. But you're very, very far from even resembling James Stewart. There's certainly no match there."

Laney wasn't so sure, however, that she didn't match Stewart's desire in a blazing dead heat.

When they finally began to eat dinner, Sandrine asked, "How was it to take over the bank business from your father?"

Laney paused because no one had ever asked. "Simple and complicated. I've worked there since I was a kid. My father would pay me to do simple things around the bank and I always felt so proud. I worked there through my teen years, then returned after getting my master's degree in finance. I knew the business inside and out, but trying to pry my father from the bank was difficult."

"He built it from scratch, yes?"

"He did. He always resisted selling to one of the conglomerates, which was trying for him, especially when the economy took a dump."

"The Bush years."

"And the Reagan years."

Sandrine paused, seeming to consider Laney. "You love your work."

"I love what my father built. And I love the community." Laney warmed to Sandrine's inquisitive eyes.

"Tell me about you, Sandrine."

"What is there to tell," she said as she appeared to gather her thoughts. "I moved from France to the United States when I graduated from high school. My parents are divorced, but I remain very close to my father. He lives just outside of Paris and is retired. Anyway, I moved to Covina and went to Westwood College and earned my bachelor's degree in criminal justice. I joined the Beverly Hills Police Department soon after and worked my way up to detective about six years ago." She flashed a grin before adding, "A case at your bank was one of my first."

"It was? Which one?"

"A mother-and-daughter team from Santa Barbara writing bad checks. They had purchased three automobiles before we caught them."

"Yes, I remember that."

"I spoke to your father then."

"I also remember you coming in not long after I took over. I think it was about a fraudulent loan application for a beauty salon that ended up really being for a brothel."

Sandrine nodded. "It was. They had applied at almost every bank in Beverly Hills. But they certainly didn't get far."

"You remembered."

"Yes."

"I'd think that a brothel would be a cash business and that they wouldn't need a loan."

"Fishnet stockings and whips are obviously more expensive than they thought."

Laney laughed. "Can your job be dangerous?"

"Sometimes. You never know how an arrest will go."

"And what about your personal life?"

"That can be dangerous, too."

"Really?"

Sandrine shrugged. "Well, in a way. I was in a serious relationship that ended badly two years ago, and since, I have been casually dating here and there. No one has made me want to have more than a few dates with them."

"So it's the same out there on the singles markets as it was four years ago before I met Judith?"

"Probably. But I can't complain. At least people accept my dinner invitations."

Sandrine smiled in a way that made Laney believe that the comment was directed at her.

"I'm glad you asked me."

Sandrine paused. "I only tell you about the dating because I like to be honest up front. But because the term *dating* can be interpreted many different ways, I can tell you that the woman I've been dating and I are going out in the true sense of just getting to know one another."

Laney felt a little relieved. "I'm dating someone else right now, too. Well, more or less."

"What does that mean, more or less?"

"It's not a traditional sort of 'Hey would you like to go out to dinner?' kind of thing. She's married."

"So you're the one with the dangerous personal life, huh?"

"Far from it. And I'm very aware that this one won't lead to the altar, that's for sure."

"I suppose not, given that she's already made that trip."

Laney was glad they were honest with each other. The air between them felt clear.

Sandrine raised her wineglass. "To new chances."

Laney raised hers and watched Sandrine's eyes sparkle. "To new chances." The tapping of their glasses together sealed their pledge.

"So," Sandrine said, "what shall we have for dessert?"

"Oh, I think I'll pass. Too many calories."

Sandrine squinted at Laney. "Be good and you will be lonely."

"That's from Mark Twain!"

"That's you as well."

"I haven't run into too many people who like Mark Twain enough to remember quotes. As a matter of fact," Laney said, as an unexpected delight filled her, "I haven't run into a single one."

"My father introduced me to his writing and I devoured everything I could find. To live in Hannibal, Missouri, and raft on the Mississippi River were my fantasies. I also wanted to end slavery."

"That must be the fighter for justice in you."

"Yes, I suppose. Twain fascinated me, especially because he

adamantly supported abolition and emancipation. Even as a child I knew those issues were politically resolved but that unjust standards remained. Just different ones."

"I love Twain," Laney said. "I even wrote a school report on him. I was supposed to analyze *The Adventures of Huck Finn* but discovered his work for women's suffrage, so I ended up reporting on his Votes for Women speech. I even wore a T-shirt to class that day that I made myself. The big red letters on it said, 'Women's rights are groovy.'"

They both laughed heartily. "Did you get an A?"

Laney shook her head. "A big fat D for not following the assignment. I wore the shirt to school for the next week in protest, and the popular girls started to hang out with me for being such a rebel."

"My Mark Twain quote is still relevant, then."

"'Be good and you will be lonely.' Yes, I suppose you're right. So, back to dessert because I'm curious. Is it true that if I try to be good and not order dessert, you'll have some of your own anyway?"

"Yes," Sandrine said. "And because you've refused dessert, I won't be able to offer you any of mine with a clear conscience."

"Ah, so that explains the 'lonely' part."

"In France, no one worries about sweets. Dessert alone isn't the enemy as long as you eat well at your regular meals."

They did order dessert, and Sandrine picked mille feuille. Laney tried the banana fritter.

"What made you decide to go to college in the U.S.?" Laney asked as she traded dessert plates with Sandrine.

"I wanted to be a law enforcement officer in the U.S. The prospect seemed more stimulating and challenging than staying in France. Actually, I was born here. My mother came to America on business while she was pregnant so I'm a legal resident. But I lived in France until I was eighteen." A sly smile drew Sandrine's lips up. "I must admit that I was swayed by all the American movies I watched as I grew up."

Laney nodded. "Fighting crime can look very romantic."

"It does for me. I knew I wouldn't be pulling a gun every day like Clint Eastwood, but I had also studied U.S. government, and I liked your political system. The way America fought for the establishment of its government in the beginning was romantic, especially the way some of the English people branched off, came to this land, and struggled to not only survive but to create a better life for themselves through self-rule."

Laney was amazed at Sandrine's insight and vision. Her depth of thought and feeling attracted Laney.

When Sandrine pulled into Laney's driveway later that night, Laney was reluctant to say good night. She was bursting with happiness and contentment. This simple, unassuming dinner had completely lifted her spirits.

She placed her hand over Sandrine's. "Tonight was wonderful, Sandrine."

"Yes, it really was. Thank you."

Sandrine caressed Laney's hand, then looked up, and her face glowed in the warm amber of the streetlights. And when Sandrine swayed toward her, Laney moved closer.

"I'd like to kiss you, Laney."

Laney smiled and closed the distance between them. The kiss was slow and beautiful. Their mouths parted slightly and Sandrine's lips were incredibly soft. When their tongues met to linger briefly, the touch was furtive and gentle.

Laney wanted to get to know Sandrine slowly. This was the perfect ending to a perfect date.

CHAPTER TEN

Kelly buzzed through to Laney's desk. "It's Theresa Aguilar."

"Thank you, Kelly." Laney picked up the receiver and punched a button on the phone. "You have impeccable timing."

"And why is that?"

"I was just thinking about how your friendship came along right when I needed it. I'm excited about all the possibilities that being connected to you will bring."

"And I am, too."

"But you didn't call me to hear me fawn over you."

"There's another party tonight."

"When do you sleep?"

"You won't want to miss this one."

"Where?"

"Ten o'clock. Three Thousand, Avenue of the Stars. The penthouse suite. Just give the security guard your name."

"Sounds good."

"It will be. I'm really looking forward to seeing you, Laney."

"It'll be great to see you, too."

"Yes, it will. The party won't start for me until I see you. Make sure you find me first."

For a while after she hung up, Laney considered Theresa's comment. Why wouldn't the party start until she arrived? And why was she supposed to find Theresa first?

Laney really should be knee-deep in a pile of paperwork she'd been neglecting but, instead, she picked up the phone.

"Hillary," she said.

"Hey, stranger."

"Yeah, I know I've been incommunicado. But I need to ask you something."

"Shoot."

"Remember Detective Girard? Sandrine Girard?"

"The cute cop you mention every time she stops by the bank?"

"Yes. Well, we had a date Saturday night."

"That's great. Isn't it?"

Laney recalled the sweet, unhurried kiss she and Sandrine had shared in the car. "It was wonderful. She's amazing and articulate. And so thoughtful."

"Well, you sound all goo-goo eyed, so I don't suppose you want to ask me if you should have another date."

"No." She squirmed in her chair. "I also might have a date tonight with Theresa."

"And the problem is?"

"I like them both. I mean, I like them in different ways, I suppose."

"You suppose?"

"Theresa, for one, isn't available. She's married."

"There's that, yes."

"But she might as well be divorced, considering her relationship with her husband."

"She is still married, though, Laney."

"I know. But finally being able to do whatever I want is fun, and I feel a little reckless. The great thing is that these women form business ventures together. They're powerful, Hillary, which is something I could really get into."

"Why wouldn't they want a bank president in their midst? You're pretty powerful yourself."

Though Laney did have considerable influence within her profession, she didn't consider herself powerful. Especially compared to women like her new friends. They not only turned heads, but they turned deals. "I'm excited about the prospect of collaborating with them. And I have to admit that where we go and the attention the group gets is exciting."

"They do get a lot of press. They're like rock stars. And now you're one of them."

Laney had to laugh. Being around Hollywood's true elite was beyond exhilarating and glamorous. "I know I shouldn't mess around with a married woman, but we're both adults."

"It's not like you'd be the first. But, Laney, why don't you focus on Sandrine. She's available, isn't she?"

"Yes, she is." Laney wondered what she was truly feeling. It was perplexing to like two women. What was the proper etiquette in this situation? Was she making too much of this? "They seem at opposite ends of the spectrum."

"Well, I suppose that's what dating's for. You're supposed to spend time with different people you're interested in and find out if you click."

"Yes, but should I date one woman at a time or date around?" She was thinking out loud now. "I mean, I don't think it'd be horrible to date around. What's the harm?"

"If they're just dates, I suppose it's fine. But if you get more intimate with one and then want to get intimate with the other, you should let them know."

"I wouldn't sleep with two women at the same time."

"Laney, you called me so I'll give you my opinion. It might be wise to avoid getting into anything with Theresa."

Laney felt like she was already traveling down that road. "That's not what I wanted to hear."

"I know that."

"But I feel, I don't know, a pull toward her. And I don't want to stop it."

Hillary sighed. "Do I have to tell you to be careful?"

"No, I know that. But that's just it, I've always been careful. My relationship with Judith was always so predictable. I want some random impulsiveness, some outlandish craziness."

"That's not you, Laney."

"But I want that. I'm bursting at the seams. My new friends

are fun and spontaneous. Theresa doesn't give a crap about rules or order."

"Just think it through, Laney."

Now Laney felt even more confused.

❖

Laney parked close to the building on Avenue of the Stars. The sheer fabric of the Alexander McQueen black cocktail dress she bought when she shopped with Kay on Melrose rippled lightly across her chest when she walked.

The security guard confirmed Laney's name on a list and showed her to an elevator. He stepped inside with her, inserted a key to unlock access to the penthouse, then exited the elevator.

As Laney rode up in silence she looked at herself in the mirrored walls and noticed that she appeared a little more pensive and full of anticipation than she wished. Blowing out a breath, she finally stepped off the lift and stopped.

A long, thickly carpeted hall led to only one place—a set of double doors at the end of the hall. Muffled music came from the other side.

She reached the door but hesitated. Theresa's words returned to her. "The party won't start for me until I see you. Make sure you find me first."

Laney checked her appearance one more time and suddenly the door opened. Dance music blared from inside as two women stumbled out—disheveled, drunk, and laughing. In the few seconds it took, Laney glimpsed what was going on inside. Something she wasn't expecting.

Women from the Pleasure Set were everywhere, kissing, fondling, and making out in pairs, in trios, in positions all over the place. The two departing women slammed the door closed, laughingly pardoned themselves to Laney, and swerved around her toward the elevator.

Laney's mind raced. She consciously tried to slow her breathing, but she knew her eyes were flung wide open.

Oh my God, she thought. *Did I just see what I thought I saw? A split-second, living snapshot of an orgy. Should I bolt? Should I go in?*

She stared at the door with a huge decision before her. *Hell, if I go home now, I might as well go over to Judith's to reconcile.* The thought was ridiculous, but this was an important juncture.

The last thing Hillary had told her was to think it through. She narrowed her eyes and, all at once, a momentous decision washed over her, burning hot in her mind as it settled in. *Who needs to think?*

❖

Laney opened the door to another burst of pulsating music. Through the hazy, dimly lit room she could make out numerous sexual liaisons. She strolled through the place, adjusting her eyes to the bodies around her. Women were everywhere, all in different stages of sex and oblivious to her. They had all been at one or more gatherings of the Pleasure Set, and now they were engaged in this outrageous orgy. She tried to act nonchalant, but surges of surprise pulsed through her as she recognized Kay Kitterman, Morgan Donnelly, and others. Bare legs, breasts, arms, asses, faces were everywhere. Everywhere.

The music changed to a techno beat, the kind she usually heard only in gay men's bars, and she understood the rationale. It was hot fuck music for hot fucking people.

She had to maneuver carefully since bodies were draped over and lying on every piece of furniture, as well as on the carpet. She made her way behind a couch sitting in the middle of the room. Someone's legs were angled in a vertical position off the back of it, causing her to have to duck to get by. She swerved to move out of the way of another couple, fervent in their movements, and was thrown off balance, half falling, half dropping to her knees to get past the maze of arms and legs. She considered standing, but it was easier to crawl, if only temporarily, to pass the jumble of bodies all around her. The beat of the music that boomed from speakers throughout the room thudded in her chest, but she could hear women close by her moaning and gasping as they rocked together in small couplings and groups.

As she crawled on all fours, trying not to look around too much, other body parts thrust and gyrated in and out of her view. Then she reached another couch against the far wall and was aware of a woman lying on it. Laney's face was even with the other woman's face, and she knew in her gut who it was before she turned.

Theresa was by herself, smiling at Laney. She wore a slinky green dress and her long legs were crossed.

They didn't say a word but their eyes immediately locked. Theresa had clearly been waiting for her. The scene was almost too insane to comprehend. Laney was on automatic pilot, no longer able to stop and consider any logical decisions, even if she knew what logic was.

Her heart beat faster, thumping in a cadence that threatened to deafen her. Desire erupted in her body as the dizzying swell of sexual stimulation overtook her. A bizarre thought hovered on the periphery of her mind. Was this what taking LSD might feel like? Her brain was sinking in a sea of erotic intoxication, powerless to surface and just as unwilling. Her limbs felt numb and she couldn't form full sentences in her mind, let alone speak out loud with any lucidity. All she could do was focus on Theresa's mouth, her lush, plump lips smiling for only her.

Still reclining, Theresa reached for Laney. She hadn't stood up yet, but somehow she glided toward the couch. Theresa drew her into a deep French kiss that was immediate and strong, sending shock waves through her body.

After some time, Theresa pulled her up onto the couch. From somewhere, she produced some Cristal champagne and they drank straight from the $500 bottle. They took turns sipping like two children who had just stolen a pitcher of Kool-Aid. They kissed and drank and kissed again, all the while never speaking.

Laney hadn't had enough champagne to feel tipsy, but the intensity of the scene went to her head immediately. It was like a sizzling, sexy dream that leaves the dreamer with panting breaths and wet thighs. Theresa pressed Laney into the couch and the bottle fell to the floor. Now on her back, Laney looked into Theresa's eyes, which were intense and provoking. She wrapped her legs around Theresa and pulled their hips together. Laney rubbed Theresa's back, feeling the warmth of her skin under the slinky fabric. When Theresa pushed her hips into Laney in rhythmic strokes, Laney moved her hands down to grip Theresa's ass, pulling her into the burning focus of her need.

Laney's mind swirled with sexual intoxication. Women were moaning around her. The murmurings of passion and the cries of orgasms intensified her rising excitement. She had heard such noises in rented porn films but had never been in the middle of such extreme sexual clamor. And as the twosomes and threesomes around them writhed and succumbed to one another, the rise and fall of the explosive unions drove Laney to a wilder and faster rhythm and she pushed her hips up into Theresa's with more intensity.

Theresa then slipped off the couch and made Laney stand in front of her as Theresa sat down again. When she hiked Laney's dress up and brusquely spread her legs, Laney saw her eyes burning darker than ever. Theresa was clearly just as horny and out of her mind as she was.

And when Theresa pushed her mouth into Laney's wetness, Laney uttered a moan so loud that, somewhere in the back of her mind, she realized she sounded like an animal in heat.

Her mind spun in crazy circles. She needed to come fast but knew somehow that Theresa wouldn't let her. Theresa's hands wrapped around her ass and her expert tongue drew Laney's clit into a hard, throbbing center of arousal. Laney opened her eyes and could make out women in the dark. They all were moving differently, stroking and humping and fondling, and the sight shot waves of stimulation through her. And when she closed her eyes, she felt only Theresa's mouth. She couldn't believe she was in a room of writhing, contorting bodies, all moaning and gasping as if to encourage each other.

Laney laid her head back and consented to the carnal onslaught.

Before long the ripples of an orgasm began to travel up her

spine. It appeared much too soon, so Laney pushed Theresa down onto her back on the couch. With Theresa's head on one end, Laney pulled her dress up and climbed on top of her in a sixty-nine position. Theresa threw one leg over the back of the couch, which offered Laney the access she craved, and she licked the dripping wetness off each thigh. Theresa shuddered at each stroke and groaned when Laney pushed her chin into Theresa's perfectly shaved center and ran her tongue over her clit a few teasing times before she plunged it inside her. Theresa spread Laney's legs and managed to continue her oral fucking while pushing her hips in rhythm with Laney's mouth.

Though Laney knew every other woman there was heavily involved in her own libidinous pursuits, she wouldn't have cared if they had all stopped to watch her. She was caught up in a wave that she refused to fight. The women were united in an erotic feast, and she blended into this setting like she had been with the group for years. She was now one of them. And she planned to get out of it what everyone else seemed to be there to get.

Theresa's thighs started shaking and Laney's flight to orgasm increased in velocity.

Abruptly Theresa moved away and Laney sat up in response. Theresa stood before her and pulled Laney forward until she sat on the front edge of the couch. She then planted her left foot up firmly on the cushion next to Laney's right hip and her right one on the ground. Theresa smiled, obviously knowing what she wanted. She must have liked this position, for she now clearly wanted Laney to do the same for her.

Theresa moved one hand behind Laney's head and pulled her into her, directing Laney's tongue between her spread legs. Laney steadied herself by wrapping her arms around Theresa's ass, which enabled her to remain locked into Theresa's clit and lips as she massaged Theresa with her mouth and tongue.

Theresa's head dropped back as she slowly began driving her hips into Laney's face.

When Theresa had been the one sitting, Laney had recognized the primal nature of the position. She felt like she was getting a blow job, which was strange but not at all objectionable. Now the restraint of Theresa's hands at the back of her head, guiding her for Theresa's maximum pleasure, sent new bolts of sexual charges through her. Theresa was grinding herself into Laney's mouth and Laney wanted it all. Feeling both dominant and submissive but completely in control, she flashed on the image of the nude women in the film they had watched.

She needed to be the vessel that carried Theresa's orgasm across the threshold. She wanted Theresa to crash into her, to pull her hair if she wanted, to dig her nails into her shoulders. Laney felt movement on the couch. Two women she didn't know very well had fallen next to her. Laney glanced to her left and saw that one was straddling the other. They were kissing passionately and gyrating together.

Theresa was moaning loudly, her head still thrown back. She either wasn't aware that these women had moved so close or didn't care.

Laney could feel the women next to her. Their hips and thighs were pressed against her and this new sensation, coupled with the realization that they were also in the midst of a sexual encounter so close that she could feel them shiver and buck, sent her libido into overdrive.

Suddenly Theresa moved away from Laney's mouth and climbed onto Laney's lap. With both their dresses pushed roughly up and out of the way, Theresa spread her legs and plunged two fingers inside Laney. Extremely wet and swollen, Laney gasped in desire, and as she accepted the strong fingers that quickly found her G-spot, she was aware that Theresa was crushing herself into the same hand. Theresa stimulated them together, and they rocked back and forth as Laney reached up and pulled Theresa's mouth to hers.

Laney was out of control. The situation was out of control. And she didn't care.

After a while with Theresa's hand stroking them both, Theresa suddenly stopped kissing her and dropped her head to Laney's shoulder. She began to alternately moan and pant. The hot breath stimulating Laney's neck made her grip Theresa's thighs to make sure she didn't move away. Laney was close to coming and tried to stay on the edge of her orgasm. But when Theresa shuddered and cried out, Laney let go. They both came loudly and with a white-hot intensity that erupted like lightning inside Laney.

CHAPTER ELEVEN

Even though Laney took a faster-than-usual shower at home, she was more than an hour late to work. Kelly eyed her suspiciously as she walked past her desk. Laney made it into her office and sat down with a heavy sigh, then dropped her forehead into her hands.

"Good morning."

Laney started, looking up to see Kelly standing at her door. "Shit," she exclaimed, her head pounding like a timpani. She was tired from no sleep and a bit rattled from her all-night experience.

Kelly lowered her voice. "Jumpy, aren't we?"

Laney began to wave her off but instead uttered one word of survival. "Coffee." She needed time to comprehend the night before. She pushed the pile of overdue paperwork away and picked up a pen, then doodled absentmindedly on a pad of paper while she reviewed last night's events.

An orgy. And she had participated with everything she had. The fact that she'd been tipsy from the champagne wasn't an excuse. As a matter of fact, it had heightened her arousal. Never had she had such raw, exposed sex. There had been no loving touches, no affectionate caresses, just feral fucking. It had thrilled and electrified her.

She had also never been among others having sex. The whole penthouse seemed to be thick with a lascivious carnal fever and she could still feel it, smell it, and taste it.

Where does it go from here? She wasn't used to having sex

for its own sake. Was that all Theresa wanted? Was that all Laney wanted? Was she making a big deal about this? Well, it *was* a big deal to her. She shook her head slowly. The Pleasure Set was more than she could have ever imagined.

Throughout the day, moments from the night before washed across her vision like little apparitions dancing to the loud drumbeats that continued to pound in her head. Bank customers walked by and she could hear the occasional buzzing of the merchant-only deposit door, but she couldn't focus on work.

Just after three p.m., Laney's cell phone rang. The caller ID showed that it was Sandrine.

Genuine attraction to this woman washed over her. But underneath the thrill of seeing Sandrine's name on her cell phone was a growing discomfort. The knowledge of the orgy the night before tainted the memory of the pleasant dinner she and Sandrine had shared. Comparing the reckless nights she had spent with Theresa to her conventional date with Sandrine confused and frustrated her. How could she be attracted to two entirely different women?

What am I doing? she asked for the first time. And in the back of her mind, she knew that the thought really applied to Theresa, not Sandrine.

As the phone chirped, Laney paused with her thumb on the Connect button. Her head pounded from fatigue, but a new dull ache throbbed in her chest. The presence of Sandrine, even via a phone connection, made Laney feel guilty and soiled. She was convinced that Sandrine would read those negative emotions in her voice and, with embarrassment, she didn't want to expose that part of herself.

She let the call go to voice mail.

❖

Later that afternoon, the office phone rang and kept ringing. Realizing that Kelly had gone to get more coffee, Laney answered it herself. "Laney DeGraff."

"Laney."

It was Theresa. Laney paused, unsure what to say.

"Sweetie," Theresa said, "are you okay?"

"What the hell happened last night?"

"You're a bit shocked, I suppose."

Kelly walked in and dropped off a mug of coffee in front of Laney. "Yes."

"It's a private thing. Just us girls, you know? Sometimes we don't get together to talk business."

Laney waited a moment for Kelly to walk out of her office. "But everyone's sleeping with everyone."

"Not really. We keep our group very confidential so feelings develop, feelings that wouldn't be safe to explore outside the group. I don't need to tell you that there would be a lot to lose if anyone— Morgan, Kay, any of us—got caught. So we stay within the circle."

"It's cheating, isn't it?"

"What, on our husbands? Boyfriends? Girlfriends? If you haven't noticed, they're fucking who they want and so are we."

"I hadn't put it in those exact words, but I suppose it was just a fuck to you."

"A figure of speech, darling. And not the most important part of what I was trying to tell you. It works, Laney. Our group works. It's no different from what most people in Hollywood are doing. We're just not hanging out at bars, getting photographed by the paparazzi and having eight-by-ten glossies show up in court. You and I are in a safe place, within a group of women that we trust."

"It's the perfect cover—"

"Divorce, for most of us, is too complicated and too costly. Everyone does it, Laney, it's just that we do it a little differently. And only with each other. We trust each other. We won't tell. We stick together and protect the group."

"I don't know what to say."

"Can you put the group aside for a moment?"

"I suppose—"

"Tell me how it felt."

"Being with you?"

"Yes."

It had been beyond belief. The sex had felt like a mind-blowing narcotic shot through her veins. She just wasn't sure if the drug was healthy. Still, the excitement was beyond anything she'd ever experienced. "Crazy. Wild."

"It was amazing for me."

"I could barely get to work."

"I can only imagine." Theresa chuckled, and then the conversation fell into a brief silence.

Theresa lowered her voice. "Will you come over to my place after work?"

Should she? Admittedly, she had never felt so free and so liberated from the oppression she had been under with Judith. What she and Theresa were doing wasn't hurting anyone. And she could compartmentalize Theresa from her job, from Sandrine, from whatever she wanted. "Yes."

❖

Felicia called while Sandrine was changing from a recent workout at the police station.

"Felicia, hello."

"Hi. What are you up to?"

"I'm about to leave the station. I'm taking the afternoon off to do some plumbing repairs at home." She pulled on a pair of Levi's.

"Sounds like loads of fun."

"It's more fun than having to go to the neighbor's house to take a shower."

Felicia laughed. "Can I talk you into lunch on the way home? I'm in between showing some properties and would love to see you."

"Sure."

"Meet me at Marix?"

"Give me a half an hour."

Marix was as busy as always. The very popular Mexican restaurant sat in the center of West Hollywood and served as a gay gathering place for the margarita-thirsty crowd. They waited twenty minutes for a table, then ordered carne asada emborrachadas.

"You look fantastic, Sandrine." Felicia gazed at her as she lifted a margarita to her lips.

"So do you, Felicia. You're dressed to kill."

"I need to. This real-estate market is threatening to murder us all."

Sandrine drank iced tea, knowing that a margarita would put her on the couch later and not in her bathroom, where the broken showerhead was waiting for her. "If I were in the market, I'd call you first."

"In the market for a house or something else?"

Sandrine responded in kind to Felicia's mischievous expression. "Why, Felicia, what could you possibly be suggesting?"

"I'm suggesting the something else. I'm nuts about you, Sandrine. You drive me crazy every time we go out. I'd like to move this to the next level."

"You mean sleep together?"

"Precisely. You'll do some harm if you don't help a girl out here." Felicia was smiling wickedly as she pinched her straw.

Sandrine wasn't opposed to having sex with Felicia, but she didn't feel enough for her to start a more intimate relationship. "We're not only talking about the next step, I suppose, but also about the next relationship step."

"Well, that'd be something we'd have to see about." Felicia squeezed Sandrine's hand. "Baby, we don't have to worry about all that serious stuff right now. I'm just saying that I'm crazy-mad attracted to you and I'd like to get to know more about that lovely body of yours."

A few weeks ago, Sandrine might not have hesitated. On a couple of occasions, they had made out heavily but stopped short of oral sex or any other kind. And while full-on sex was the next logical step, Sandrine wanted to take one thing into account.

"Before we go any further with this conversation, Felicia, just so you know, I went on a date the other night."

"That's great." Felicia nodded. "You know I date others too."

"I do."

"So, I'm a little confused, baby. What bearing does your other date have on us?"

Suddenly Sandrine wasn't quite sure. Her reasoning had sounded coherent in her head. She had finally gotten to take Laney out, and that opportunity had been a long time coming for her. But in actuality, Laney was dating others as well. Maybe she was making too big a deal out of Laney too soon. She seemed to be going against her own credo—to let dating be just that.

"I suppose it doesn't. I just thought you should know."

"Well, thanks for telling me. Now let's get back to a much more appealing conversation. Let's talk about you."

Sandrine laughed. "What do you want to know that you haven't already asked?"

"You haven't told me much about your work."

"You know what I do."

"But is it exciting? Do you get to use your handcuffs and your gun?" Felicia wiggled her eyebrows up and down.

"No more margaritas for you, lady," Sandrine joked. "Yes, I use my cuffs a lot and no, I haven't used my gun."

"Is that typical?"

"It is. Our guns are a last resort. We have many ways to apprehend a bad guy that lethal force, especially in my department, is rare."

"You know, I've never seen you in uniform."

"That's because I'm a detective and we don't wear uniforms."

"Well, you look good. I tell you, you dress well enough to sell real estate."

"Thank you, Felicia."

"No need to thank me. I call it like I see it."

After lunch, Sandrine walked Felicia to her car. She had parked a couple blocks up Flores Street, and when they reached the Lexus, Sandrine hugged her good-bye.

Felicia got into her car, started the engine, and rolled down the window. "Thank you for meeting me, Sandrine."

Sandrine bent over and placed her hands on the window frame. "I had a very nice time with you."

She kissed Felicia. Though she didn't intend it to be a deep kiss, when Felicia's arms wrapped around her to pull her closer, it became more serious. Sandrine was aware that her ass was sticking out into the street and just before she broke away, Felicia moved her hand around to the front of Sandrine's shirt and, with a few clever twists of the wrist, she ducked inside and under Sandrine's bra.

The swift onset, followed by a gentle pinch of her already hardening nipple, made Sandrine gasp. She pulled her lips away from Felicia's, and they stared at one another while Felicia continued to massage Sandrine's breast. When one of the many passing cars blew its horn, Felicia's lips curved into a smile.

"Mercy."

Felicia blew out a breath.

Sandrine looked down the street and back. "You might want to remove your hand from my breast now."

Felicia laughed and did so. "You be careful with that plumbing job, Detective."

"I will."

As Felicia pulled out of her parking spot she said, "See you again soon, I hope."

Sandrine straightened up and waved halfheartedly as Felicia drove off. She didn't have to wonder why she didn't feel more enthusiastic.

Hillary didn't look too happy as she lunched with Laney at Patina.

"I haven't heard much from you lately."

"I know." Laney pushed her fork around a Cobb salad, not hungry in the slightest. "I've been really busy."

"With Sandrine?"

"No, not really. I mean, we had a date. It was amazing." Laney wasn't sure what she was doing. She really liked Sandrine, but she was distracted because she was spending so much time with Theresa.

"But…" Hillary coaxed her.

"Things happened last night."

"With Sandrine?"

"No. With Theresa."

"You mean you kissed her?"

"A little more than that."

"You had sex?"

"More than that."

Hillary stopped eating and placed her own fork down. "What could be more than that?"

"It was an orgy."

Silent for a few beats, Hillary raised her eyebrows. "Wow. I didn't see that one coming."

"Neither did I. It was crazy. I mean, I expected something to happen because of the way Theresa posed the invitation to the party. I just didn't expect such a scene."

"So you hooked up with a lot of women?"

"No, just Theresa. I mean everyone was with someone, or two someones. I don't know. Once Theresa and I got together, I wasn't aware of much else. Just a lot of bodies and noises. Sex noises."

"Holy crap. An orgy." Hillary sat back in her chair. "I thought most of these women were straight."

"They are. I mean, outwardly. Maybe they're bisexual. But they don't really live a bisexual life. Most of them are married. I don't know. It's a little confusing."

"You need to be careful, Laney. I'm not sure you know what you're getting into."

Laney *was* a little concerned, but she just didn't want to drive down the safe and boring road anymore. "Judith sucked the life out of me, and before that, I always seemed to get with people who were too damn predictable. Theresa's just the opposite. She's exciting."

"It's just that I've seen a change in you recently. We hardly talk anymore. You haven't seen Isabelle in a long time. And you yourself have said that you've been out until all hours of the night for a lot of nights in a row."

Laney was aware of that fact and also aware that she'd been coming in late to work the past week. That was so unlike her. She felt off balance and a little apprehensive about what people might think. She certainly hadn't been a good friend to Hillary recently. But damn it, she was finally living.

"The other end of my candle has never burned. I can handle it, Hill."

CHAPTER TWELVE

Theresa's house was nestled in the Holmby Hills section of Los Angeles, an affluent neighborhood situated between the equally wealthy districts of Beverly Hills and Westwood.

In an ultramodern kitchen, with high-end appliances and hand-carved cabinetry made from exotic wood, Laney sat in a sleek, chocolate-colored leather and chrome designer chair. Theresa had just finished uncorking a bottle of wine when a woman in a maid's uniform walked in.

"Anything else, Mrs. Aguilar?"

"No, Dahlia. See you tomorrow."

The woman left and from somewhere in the house, a door clicked closed.

Theresa poured the wine into two crystal Riedel Sommelier wineglasses. "So tell me about work." She handed Laney a glass and stepped back to the kitchen counter to rest against it.

"What about it?"

"Your day. How was it?"

"Well, after I finally had some caffeine and an aspirin, I was able to tackle the usual affairs. Barely. I had to polish a set of documents on legal and regulatory banking requirements for our corporate office. Pretty boring stuff."

"I wouldn't say a president's job is boring."

"Well, it is."

"You're in charge of security, large sums of money, high-stakes business transactions—"

"Boring."

"I think it's quite exciting." Theresa put down the wineglass and walked over to Laney. "I think you're exciting."

She stood over her and took a strand of Laney's hair in her hands. Laney closed her eyes for a moment. *This is kind of crazy,* she thought. Her heart raced, but not purely from excitement. *Theresa is married. I'm in her house after having sex with her last night.* She shook inside at the perverse notion that, while being at the Tire Store or the Penthouse was fairly secure in its privacy, being in the house Theresa shared with her husband felt hazardous.

When she opened her eyes, Theresa was regarding her intensely. She then knelt between Laney's legs. They kissed passionately, the sweet blackberry taste from the Chateau Margaux on their lips.

Theresa hiked Laney's skirt up and worked her mouth down along Laney's body, stopping between her legs. Silently Theresa pulled Laney's legs apart and then toward her so that her ass rested on the edge of the chair. In this slouched position, Laney spread her legs to allow Theresa's kneeling form to fit between them. Theresa kissed her again, licking and sucking Laney's tongue and lips. Theresa's quiet moans shot lightning bolts through Laney's head. Theresa didn't waste much time moving down between her legs once more. When she pulled Laney's panties to the side, the immediate hot surge of Theresa's tongue slammed through Laney's body.

It was still light out and Laney was edgy about the large picture windows behind Theresa. Though her head spun at the blatant, mind-blowing seduction, Laney's nervousness escalated. Anyone could walk by and look in.

Laney let her head fall back but the desire to watch what Theresa was doing and the necessity of keeping an eye on the windows made her lift her head often. The sensation of Theresa between her legs, essentially servicing her, was wicked and electrifying. In this position, she could only call up images of women going down on men, and Theresa's head was moving in just that way. The positions they had been in at the orgy, and now this one, seemed almost pornographic, and she was surprised when the thought made her even wetter and hornier.

Laney knew she wouldn't last long. Seeing the powerful, always-in-control Theresa kneeling between her legs, her hair lying disheveled on Laney's thighs, was just too much visual stimulation. She let herself go and an incredibly strong orgasm ripped through her, making her grip the back of the chair and push herself into Theresa's face.

As she bucked from the unbelievable contractions, a faint humming noise filtered through Laney's consciousness—the sound of a car pulling into the garage. Laney tried to stop, grabbing Theresa's shoulders, but Theresa refused.

Someone would be walking into the house, and the tension of knowing she and Theresa were seconds from getting caught tore at her brain while not wanting Theresa to stop tore at her body. As if she knew the exact number of seconds she had left, Theresa moved away from her and stood up just as a key clicked in the kitchen's back-door lock.

Laney pushed her skirt down as Theresa's husband strode through the door. He was on his cell phone, in the middle of a conversation about golf. Theresa had gracefully turned toward the counter and was acting neither shocked, fearful, nor guilty.

"Theresa," her husband said, nodding that he was on the phone.

"Hello, Roger. Meet Laney DeGraff."

"Hang on, Rich," Roger said as he walked past and looked down at Laney. "Pleasure."

Theresa took a sip from her wineglass and they both watched as Roger's gaze swept from Theresa to Laney and back to Theresa. Theresa stared indifferently.

"Dinner at La Scala at eight," Roger said as he made his way out of the kitchen.

"Of course," Theresa responded.

Laney's heart was pounding and her mind raced in fight-or-flight readiness. She had held her breath while Roger was in the room so he wouldn't notice that she was panting from the last trembling contractions of her orgasm, but now she blew out the breath and stared at Theresa, who merely smiled back.

❖

Wednesday morning was slow at the bank, so Laney was surprised when Kelly made a loud "Psssst!" sound in her direction.

Kay Kitterman had walked in and was talking to a customer-service rep. The bank customers, as well as the tellers, had all turned their attention to her. No one moved for a few seconds. Laney had to stifle a laugh since it looked like the bank had gone into a time freeze. After being pointed toward Laney's office, Kay nodded her thanks and strode over. Laney met her at the office door and they hugged. Laney asked Kelly for some coffee and Kelly jumped up from her desk, eyebrows raised in surprise.

"Laney, I'm so glad you're in." Kay took an offered chair at Laney's desk.

"Don't tell me you want to go shopping again," Laney joked. "I'm tied up here until after five, plus my checkbook couldn't take another onslaught."

"No, silly. I'd like to open an account."

"You, too?"

"Theresa recommended it. She liked the way you handled her." Laney knew what Kay's sly grin really meant.

Laney decided to ignore the jest and opened her drawer to pull out a form. "Well, then, let's get you started."

As she did with Theresa, she helped Kay fill out the form and asked, "What will the opening balance be?"

Kay reached into her purse and withdrew a large stack of one-hundred-dollar bills. "Twelve thousand."

While that amount was not unusual in Beverly Hills, Laney said, "I do need to inform you that standard policy requires that we report anything over ten thousand."

"Oh. Well, I don't want any reporting. No one needs to know my business. I'll deposit nine thousand, then."

"Fine." They chatted while Laney completed the forms and gave Kay her copies. After no more than fifteen minutes, Laney walked her to the bank's front door.

As Laney opened it for her, Kay lowered her voice. "You asked me a while ago why we're called the Pleasure Set."

Laney nodded.

"They think we're all about hedonistic shopping sprees and expensive dinners out. You know the real meaning now. It's funny how close they are to the truth." Kay kissed her on the cheek. "If they only knew." She waved and turned south on the boulevard.

❖

After picking up Sandrine's voice mail saying that she'd had a nice time at dinner, Laney returned her call, apologizing for taking so long.

"It was lovely for me, too, Sandrine." Laney had truly enjoyed their time. Dinner had been full of great conversation, and Sandrine had listened so intently. She had made Laney feel important, and she had found it easy to tune into Sandrine as well. They had a strong connection when they were together. Laney had thought it was just a work-related thing, but now she knew better.

Laney waved off another call that Kelly was trying to forward to her. "You know, I really like you."

"You do?"

Laney could hear the gentle teasing in Sandrine's voice. "I do."

"Well, that would be a good thing because I have a huge crush on you."

"Just a crush?"

"Much more, I have to admit."

"Then I hope that means that you won't think me too forward by asking you to go out to dinner with me again."

"That would be fantastic," Sandrine said. "I'm working on a few cases, but I'll have some free nights toward the weekend."

"Shall we plan on Friday night around seven? I'll pick you up this time."

"It sounds perfect. And if I didn't have all this work staring at me, I'd beg you to make it sooner."

"Can't the criminals just wait?"

Sandrine laughed. "If it could only be that easy to push off work for another perfect evening with you."

A flash of passion raced through Laney's chest. Sandrine was so direct and wore her emotions and feelings on her sleeve. And she was always incredibly sexy.

"You're going to make me fall hard for you, Detective."

"Would that be a crime?" Sandrine almost pulled off the remark but sniggered.

"Ha! You're not only smart but you can turn a great pun."

"Puns and guns, that's me."

Since Sandrine had chosen Crustacean for their first date, which was an ideal restaurant, Laney said, "I'd like to pick the next restaurant. Is that okay?"

"Fantastic," Sandrine said. "I'm really looking forward to it. Let me give you my address."

As Laney hung up, she sat back in her chair, thrilled about their upcoming dinner date. Admittedly, she felt awkward dating two people at the same time, but she wanted to go with the flow and see what went where. She didn't have to be in love with Theresa to continue seeing her, but she sure had wild times with her. Her body felt alive in so many extraordinary ways.

But being with Sandrine felt distinctively genuine and real. And while she and Sandrine had not connected physically, she felt emotionally alive when she was around her. The feelings that Sandrine caused inside her spoke volumes. Just being with her was better than almost anything she could imagine.

❖

"Are you freakin' crazy?" Hillary was almost yelling into the phone as Laney changed from her business suit to a deep sea blue Marc Jacobs dress. She had gotten home from work with just enough time to shower and change. "Theresa's husband could have killed you!"

"Don't you think I know that?" Laney had been virtually petrified when Roger walked through the door. Surely they were both flushed from the sex. It had to have been obvious. She prayed Roger had been too wrapped up in his phone conversation to notice. And when Theresa had called to tell her to meet the group down at the Tire Store later that evening, she neither alluded to any confrontation with her husband nor sounded stressed.

"I'm not crazy about your new friend," Hillary said. "She's running on a different kind of octane."

It felt like nitroglycerin. "I'm having fun and I can handle myself, Hill."

"At the risk of sounding like your nagging mother, I'm not so sure. And at the risk of sounding like the nagging mother I am, you still haven't taken Isabelle out for ice cream. You used to see her all the time, Laney. I'm just concerned that things have really changed. And I'm not sure for the better. You're running with a hard-hitting crowd."

Laney couldn't disagree, but this change was good for her. "I'll take Isabelle out soon."

CHAPTER THIRTEEN

When Laney arrived at the Tire Store, about eight women from the Pleasure Set were there. It was just after ten p.m. and they were already enjoying some scrumptious-looking cocktails.

Theresa handed her a drink. "Don't get too comfortable. This is just a stopover."

"Where are we going?"

"A new location."

"Really?" What creative pursuit did she have in mind this time?

They hung out for about a half an hour, Laney mostly talking to Kay as Theresa gently rubbed Laney's thigh while conversing with a woman named Sandy. Theresa finally stood. "Grab your car keys and a bottle of your choice, girls, we're going out. Laney, you can ride with me."

"Whose car is this?" Laney had never seen Theresa driving the red Mercedes they climbed into.

"My husband's."

"Didn't you have plans with your husband tonight?"

"Yes. Dinner. He's home now, passed out drunk for the rest of the night."

They drove through Beverly Hills and down Rodeo Drive. The businesses were all closed, and Laney had just begun to wonder where they would end up when Theresa parked down the block from the First Bank of Rodeo. Then a few other cars carrying their friends parked in curbed spaces behind them.

"I hope you have your keys," Theresa said as she turned off the engine.

"My keys?"

"Time to party at your place."

"Theresa, this isn't a good idea. There are security cameras in the building, you know that."

"Turn them off."

"I can't do that."

"You're the president, Laney. You can do what you want."

"It's highly against the rules."

Theresa turned toward Laney. "That's why it's called fucking the system. Most people can't get away with the things we can. But we can because we're in the correct, say, social position. It's truly harmless, though. We just want to get together in different places and party. You'll be there to make sure we don't do anything detrimental. We always do this. No big deal."

Laney didn't like the idea at all, but maybe she was playing it too safe. Besides, no one looked at the security footage unless Laney authorized it, and that was only if there was reason to.

A niggling concern lodged in the pit of her stomach. Should she propose that they just go somewhere else? The women wouldn't like such a suggestion. No one ever seemed to worry about what they did or where they went. They all seemed to have a fearlessness that she longed to have. They had an unruffled fuck-it-all demeanor and people stepped out of their way. So what harm could a little time in the bank do?

"Let me switch off the motion detectors and cameras first."

Laney unlocked the rear door of the bank. The women filed into the back foyer and Laney told them to stay there while she turned toward the security equipment housed in a metal box on the wall. She opened the cover with her key, then hesitated.

Theresa stepped up behind her, and when Laney glanced over her shoulder, Theresa smiled her encouragement. *It'll just be a little while*, she told herself. She punched in the code to disarm the alarm. Next, she needed to turn the cameras off. She paused, thinking about how important the security cameras were. Each night, a specially formatted tape was marked with the day's date and inserted into the recorder. Since a time-code mark was registered in the top right corner of the image, a turned-off tape would contain a noticeable skip.

If no one ever requested the tapes for that night, no one would ever know they were turned off for a while. And even then, she reassured herself that she could explain away the "accidental deactivation" with an innocent story about coming in to work late and inadvertently hitting the wrong button. The First Bank of Rodeo's record had always been squeaky clean, and no one would question a chance mistake by a very tired bank president who was the daughter of the founder.

She removed some blank tapes that lay on top of the recorder, ready for the next few days of recording, and placed them off to the side so she could access the Record button. She took a deep breath and pushed the red button that disabled the cameras. When the red light next to the button went dark, she turned to the women.

"Let's just stay in my office. The security company that drives by doesn't need to see us lounging around by the front door."

"Fair enough," Theresa said.

They all moved to Laney's office, where they opened bottles of wine and champagne, and Laney turned her computer on to play music.

Theresa kissed Laney on the cheek, saying, "I have to pee. Be right back. And don't worry, I'll be inconspicuous."

When Theresa returned, Laney saw her standing in the doorway assessing the women clumped together in her office, sharing the few chairs that were there and sitting on the desk and credenza. "It's too cramped in here, ladies. Let's move this party to a bigger room."

More than a few concurred, but as they were getting up to head for the door, Laney spoke up, "I'm not crazy about this. We're nice and secluded back here."

"We could move it to the vault," Theresa said.

"Yeah, Laney," Morgan was starting to slur, "loosen up a little. We just want to see where the money from our new business venture will be living."

"And besides," Theresa added, "the cameras are off." She reached for Laney's hand.

Trepidation shimmered down her spine, but Laney knew the roving security patrols wouldn't be able to see into the vault, so she switched off her computer and office lights, took Theresa's hand, and led them there.

Lined with tall rows of brushed-steel safety-deposit boxes, the vault didn't provide anywhere to sit except an empty rolling cart used for heavy items and bags of money. A few women perched on it, passing a bottle of Enate Uno Chardonnay back and forth. Theresa led Laney to a corner of the vault and pushed her up against the deposit boxes, crushing her with a kiss. Theresa's lips were plump and hot, and Laney could taste cranberry red lipstick sweetened by champagne.

Other women coupled up and did the same, pressed to the walls, standing with legs entwined, making out and fondling. Sounds of women kissing echoed through the chamber, and Kay's words about the Pleasure Set came to Laney's mind. *If they only knew.*

Laney and Theresa kissed for a long time, rubbing their hips into one another and massaging each other's shoulders and backs. Surprising thoughts wandered through Laney's mind. She would never fall in love with Theresa, though Theresa was unbelievably hot and sexy. It was not necessarily because Theresa was married but because Laney simply hadn't experienced the growing affection and the eventual desire to share tenderness and devotion that usually followed the physical lure. This was just sex. And that thought astonished her the most. She had never "just had sex."

Theresa had not mentioned words like *lover* or *relationship* to Laney. It was true that being with Theresa was exciting and provocative. But it was also one-sided.

Being with Theresa was fun. However, it was always when Theresa planned it. Laney wasn't free to stop by Theresa's house, and after the close call with her husband, she wouldn't want to. And tonight was a little too much for Laney. She really didn't want to be at the bank. She was taking a huge risk and was uncomfortable because she was worried. Why couldn't they simply hang out like normal people? A restaurant here, a movie there. But the Pleasure Set wasn't interested in being normal. They had to be somewhat clandestine, given some of the activities they indulged in. Plus, they considered normal to be a dreadfully humdrum and inferior lifestyle.

She liked the group of women, but each gathering was a surreal experience that was orchestrated primarily by Theresa.

At the moment that it was becoming very apparent to Laney that the affair would never go anywhere, Theresa moved her hand down to slip under Laney's dress. The realization came with a gradual fizzle and a halting sputter. Laney had begun to slowly squirm away from Theresa's hand when a loud crash made her jump.

Kay had knocked a bottle of wine off the rolling cart and it had broken into a few large pieces on the cement floor. "Shit!" Kay yelped. "I'm sorry!"

Luckily, there wasn't much liquid left and the white wine probably wouldn't stain.

Theresa quickly moved away. "I'll get some paper towels." And she had left before Laney could offer to go instead. Laney carefully picked up the pieces of glass and carried them to the wastebasket in her office. On occasion she had opened a bottle of congratulatory wine or Scotch with affluent customers, so she was sure no one would question the sodden remains.

Laney met Theresa on the way back to the vault. Together they cleaned up the mess, and though the wine smelled slightly pungent, it was strongest when she was kneeling close to the floor. She hoped the bank staff wouldn't notice traces of the incident. And even though a mini-calamity was diverted, that was exactly the kind of problem Laney had feared would crop up.

"Okay, ladies," Theresa said after the damp paper towels had also been deposited in Laney's trash can, "we'd better wrap this up before someone spills something else that's more expensive or leaves more of a stain."

It was a little past one a.m. when Laney turned the cameras and alarm system back on. She locked up and Theresa drove her to the Tire Store to retrieve her car.

During the ride back, Laney thought about how she could gracefully back out of the intimacy with Theresa but keep the business relationship intact.

"I want a rain check on what we were interrupted doing," Theresa said as she parked the red Mercedes parallel to Laney's car.

Laney forced a smile and reached for the door.

"Tomorrow night is an art opening at Morgan's art gallery," Theresa said. "It's a big event. See you there?"

"Sure," Laney replied.

"My husband will be with me. I wanted you to know so you wouldn't be surprised."

"Thanks for letting me know." It did surprise her a little. Although Theresa was married, she rarely seemed to be with Roger. Laney was slightly surprised that she didn't feel very jealous. And at that moment, she felt strangely relieved that she wouldn't be risking any surreptitious trysts tomorrow night. Of course, she never knew what was up Theresa's sleeve. She could be planning a rendezvous in the art gallery's broom closet, which Laney needed to avoid. She had already experienced one brush with discovery by Roger, and she sure didn't want to flirt with disaster a second time. She had done more risky things in the past days than in her entire previous life.

As she drove home, she experienced an invigorating energy. She was relieved that they were out of the bank but also felt a dizzying recklessness at what they had just done. She was truly part of the Pleasure Set now. After things cooled with Theresa, she imagined that Theresa would still be okay. Then they could focus on all the great business deals that would develop. What they did was no one else's business. No one would understand. She surely wouldn't have before she became part of the group.

For that reason, it was probably smart to keep any further details from Hillary.

❖

Felicia opened Sandrine's bottle of Château Beychevelle and carried it over to the fireplace, then reclined on some large stuffed floor pillows with Sandrine.

"I know it's not winter," Felicia filled Sandrine's glass, "but a fire always makes my place feel cozier." She filled her own glass and set the bottle down on the hearth.

The warmth of the fire did feel inviting, and Sandrine toasted Felicia. "Salut."

"Salut," Felicia said. "This is nice."

Sandrine took a sip. "It is."

Before long, the bottle was almost empty and Felicia and Sandrine were laughing about a favorite television show they both watched.

"If it wasn't for Shane and Alice, I wouldn't have watched it at all. They made it much more interesting. And I'm glad Jenny got her just reward."

"Oh, I liked Jenny. She was so horrible in such a fun way," Felicia said.

"She was awful all the time."

"But the actress was so good playing that role. Actually, she was brilliant, because she made us hate her character so much."

"I see what you mean. She must be a great actress because she made me cringe every time she was on screen."

Felicia placed her wineglass on the hearth. "Yes, that was her talent."

Felicia took Sandrine's wineglass and set it next to hers. "And you have a lot of talent, too." She kissed Sandrine full on the mouth.

The wine had loosened Sandrine up quite a bit and she went with the feeling of Felicia's lips and tongue and roaming hands. When Felicia laid her back, Sandrine felt the full weight of her and moved her hips until they were in line underneath Felicia's. She pushed up, and Felicia moaned and ground her hips back into Sandrine's. Felicia was quick to get excited and Sandrine had found out that almost anything stimulated her.

As they made out, Felicia breathed more rapidly. "I need you to touch me," she said, and grabbed Sandrine's hand, pushing it down her pants. This wasn't the first time they had ventured that far, but before they had merely massaged each other without climaxing. This time, however, Felicia seemed hell-bent on getting there.

Sandrine followed Felicia's movements, finding the right spots at the right times. Felicia moaned and grew wetter as she gyrated on top of her. As they were kissing, the thought of kissing Laney jumped into Sandrine's mind. Surprised, she let the thought linger. Imagining Laney kissing her and feeling the stimulation against her pelvic bone made her grow wet from the fantasy and awkward from the guilt.

When Felicia began to shudder, Sandrine's fantasy evaporated. And as much as she now wanted to stop what she was doing, she knew that would be cruel. She slowed her movement down, though keeping the same pressure.

Felicia screamed and bucked several times during her orgasm.

As Felicia's body wound down and her cooing subsided, Sandrine thought again about where she was and what she was doing. She liked Felicia but didn't feel the connection she desired. The experience had left her aroused, but she didn't feel like having Felicia reciprocate. She just wanted to go home.

They kissed a while longer and when Felicia began to unbutton Sandrine's Levi's, Sandrine gently covered her hands with her own.

"What's the matter, baby?" Felicia rose to look her in the eyes.

"I'm good. I just don't feel like going any further tonight."

"Is everything all right?"

"Yes, most definitely."

Felicia smiled faintly. "Might this have to do with the new date?"

Sandrine returned the smile. "I suppose it does."

"Well, I won't take it personally. I've felt that before with others. It's part of the dating game. But I have to say that you're just about the sexiest women I've seen in a long while."

"Thank you, Felicia. Could we just hang out, enjoy the fire, and talk?"

"As long as you do one thing." Felicia put her arm around her. "Don't forget about me if things change."

CHAPTER FOURTEEN

All the parking spaces on Melrose Avenue were full when Laney arrived at the Morgan Art Gallery so she parked on a side street, almost two blocks away. She had to wait in a long line to get in, and a group of paparazzi stood on either side of the doorway snapping photographs as people entered and calling out the names of the many celebrities that were there.

Eventually, she got inside and mingled with the crowd until Kay grabbed her arm.

"We're all in the back," she said, and led Laney to a group of Pleasure Set women and some men she didn't recognize. She met Morgan Donnelly's husband as well as Kay's actor boyfriend, Rance, which was odd because Laney thought Kay had broken up with him. Someone handed Laney a glass of champagne while Morgan explained that she had successfully procured the artwork of a famous Russian artist whose name was so long Laney couldn't easily repeat it.

Later that evening, she spotted Theresa and Roger through the crowd. Theresa was wearing a dark blue strapless dress with a rather large sparkling diamond necklace. She looked ravishing. Theresa glanced her way and smiled just as Roger's hand settled on her shoulder.

"Not as much fun as the Tire Store, is it?"

Laney turned to meet the million-dollar smile of Candace Dooring. Other than being involved in a few group chats, Laney hadn't talked much to the TV star.

"Candace, hello," she said.

"Stag tonight?"

"Yes."

"Me, too. I don't have a husband to drag around. As a matter of fact, I don't even have a wife to drag around. But it's all good."

Laney laughed. "Neither do I."

"Especially with Roger here." Candace lifted her chin toward Theresa. "She sure has her sights set on you."

"She does?"

"She hasn't focused that much attention on anyone in a while. I'm just not sure that's a good thing," she said, and shrugged in an odd way. "But you're safe tonight. Wifely duties call. I heard you all had fun at the bank the other night."

Laney's heart stopped for a millisecond. "You heard we were there?"

Candace nodded. "Fucking the system. Don't worry. No one talks outside the group. That's the problem."

The reassurance made her feel a little better, but Candace's last words were a bit cryptic.

"You should be careful," Candace added. "The Pleasure Set is more than you might think."

"What do you mean?"

Candace's eyes darted left and right abruptly. "I stopped going. There's something—"

Morgan walked up.

"Hello, ladies." Morgan placed her hand on Candace's shoulder. "Having a nice time?"

"Yes," Laney replied.

"Candace, we haven't seen you out in a while. Everything okay?"

Candace wouldn't look at Morgan and stared straight ahead toward Laney. "I've been working."

Morgan smiled and squeezed her shoulder. "Well, let's hope we see you soon." She nodded to Laney and meandered away.

Candace gulped down the rest of her drink. Laney couldn't ascertain the source of the tension and wasn't sure she should bring it up because Candace seemed very apprehensive now. Changing the subject might help. "So, what have you been working on?"

"A television series called *Cyber High*. It's popular with the pre-teen crowd. We're mini-gods to anyone under thirteen."

Laney wondered what Candace's producers would think if they knew about her partying with the Pleasure Set. Worse yet, she wondered what the pre-teens would think.

They stayed in back by the open bar and talked for another half an hour or so. It was too crowded for Laney to even try to make her way around to see the paintings hanging on the walls, so getting to know Candace was fine with her.

She hadn't spoken with Theresa, whom she'd lost sight of right after Theresa smiled at her. A few of the Pleasure Set women had ambled by to say hi while refreshing their drinks, and finally, around ten thirty, she told Candace she would be leaving.

"I'll walk out with you," Candace said. "But I'm afraid the paparazzi may get pushy. I hope you don't mind."

Mind? Probably half of her friends and all of her coworkers would love for the paparazzi to hassle them. "Let's go."

Out on the street, cameras flashed and people hollered, "Candace, over here!" as they made their way through the crowd.

Pushing through the throng of camera-jockeying people was daunting as Laney and Candace were swarmed and jostled. Candace slipped her arm through hers and gripped her tight. Everywhere Laney looked, flashes burst in her eyes. She had seen Candace's pictures in magazines and now the famous actress was holding on to her. The paparazzi were on both sides of them, those in front of them walking backward as they called out Candace's name.

Candace told her to keep pushing through and didn't let go until the paparazzi finally retreated a couple of blocks down the street.

"Thanks, Laney," Candace said as she retrieved her car keys from her purse. "Can I give you a lift to your car?"

"No, I'm just a block or two that way."

"Okay, then. And Laney..." Candace hesitated. She suddenly looked scared. "Be careful."

Candace's lips parted again and Laney leaned closer to hear

the words that were forming, but instead a subtle grimace washed across Candace's face and her mouth clamped shut.

Laney watched Candace unlock the door and climb into her Lexus. Why did Candace's concern seem so dire?

❖

Laney had been to the O-Bar on Santa Monica Boulevard many times. The designers had hit all their marks in creating an elegant dining atmosphere. Just the right elements of fabric, stone, water, wood, and fire in both their dining room and popular Forbidden Garden made this the perfect atmosphere to share with Sandrine.

The server brought Laney the fettuccini and wild mushroom pasta, and Sandrine chose the pan-roasted salmon.

"Try this." The forkful Sandrine offered Laney tasted delightful.

They shared bites and light conversation until dinner was almost over. Laney loved hearing about Sandrine's life. She was viewing a more detailed picture of who this wonderful woman was. Sandrine was as delightful as usual, and even the small talk at the beginning of dinner was enjoyable and full of wit and appeal.

It was easy to open up to Sandrine, and after dinner, Laney asked her to go for a drink in the garden. As the servers came to take their dishes, Laney ordered red wine to be brought outside.

O-Bar's outside Forbidden Garden area was as magnificent as the dining area, with the added bliss of seventy-degree weather. The night had cooled and a light desert breeze ruffled the fabric-shade structures. With up-lit palm trees, flickering candles, and grassy islands divided by stone pathways, the Forbidden Garden embodied elegance and relaxation.

They sat toward the back on a wicker sofa punctuated with plush caramel-colored pillows. As they drank their wine, Laney let her head fall back and looked at the stars.

"How have you been all these long days since we last had dinner?" Sandrine asked.

"Well, I haven't seen you, which is a bummer." Laney grinned and watched Sandrine's mouth turn up into a smile as well. "But otherwise, things have been exciting and a little crazy." Laney didn't want to share the details with Sandrine; it would definitely not be appropriate. But she didn't want Sandrine to misunderstand their time together. "This date, however, has been the most enjoyable one I've had in a long time."

"Not exciting, you mean?" Sandrine's sly grin let Laney know she was kidding.

"A different kind of exciting."

"And certainly not crazy," Sandrine said. "I hope."

"You hope?"

"A crazy date. You know, the kind that makes you look at your watch and wonder if you'll ever get home without the police getting involved."

Laney laughed. "So you've had those kinds of dates?"

"Yes." Sandrine sipped her wine.

"You have to tell me."

"Once," Sandrine began, "I was on a date with a woman whom I had met at an organic food store. We decided to go out for dinner, so we went to a restaurant in town and five minutes into the main entrée she took off her jacket. What she had on underneath, let me just say, was more revealing than is acceptable in public."

"Really?"

"Yes. It was a silk tank top with the armholes cut so low you could see the skin of her waist. She wasn't wearing a bra, and when she gestured, everything jiggled around and sometimes wiggled right out."

"Wow."

"When too much of her breasts started popping out, the manager came over and asked her to cover up."

"Did she?"

"Not only did she not, she got so incensed that she stood up and pulled her tank top off."

Laney laughed and Sandrine joined her. "She said, 'This is me and this is a natural thing, a thing of beauty.'"

"No, she didn't!"

"Yes. I tried to convince her to cover up, too, but she yelled, 'This is for you! I'm beautiful and special and I want you to see me!'" Sandrine paused. "Of course, everyone else could see her, too, so it wasn't that special in my book."

Laney laughed even harder. "I take it that was your last date?"

"Oh, yes. I made her leave before the restaurant could call the police. With my luck, someone I know would have shown up, and then I would have been the butt of jokes at the station for a long time."

"I remember once," Laney said when the laughter died down a little, "I was on a blind date that a coworker set up. When she picked me up, she was driving a hearse."

"Like a vintage hearse converted into a classic car?"

"No. Like a working hearse with the mortuary name on the side. She explained that she worked at a funeral home and needed to drop by work really quick before our dinner. When we arrived, she parked out back and invited me in. She gave me a quick tour, which was a little weird, but I was thinking, hey, everybody has a job, and the business of dead people is a job."

Sandrine chuckled. "I'm not sure I like where this is going."

"You'd be right. She kept stalling and I got a little creeped out. Then the back door buzzed and she answered it. Some paramedics were wheeling in a gurney with a body on it. She apparently had been paged on the way over to my house to receive a new, ah, client."

"No!"

"Yes. I waited in the chapel while she did whatever she had to with the body, and after a long while, she came in apologizing for the delay. She said that since we had missed our dinner reservations, she'd ordered pizza in."

"In the mortuary?"

Laney rolled her eyes and nodded. "She had set up a table and we ate dinner with about twenty dead bodies."

Sandrine's genuine-sounding belly laugh warmed Laney's heart. "I suppose romance was hard to come by with all those people so near."

"It was nonexistent. I could barely gulp down the pepperoni before I pretended to be tired so she would take me home."

Laney and Sandrine continued to share funny stories on the drive back to Sandrine's. When they pulled into the driveway, Laney turned off the engine and they sat there until the laughing died down.

"You mentioned earlier that your last serious relationship ended badly."

Sandrine nodded. "It did."

"What happened?"

"I met Chris, my ex, when she was at UCLA studying for her master's degree. Things were good at the beginning, but I sensed that she had an edge that she hadn't really shown. She would go off into some dark mental place at times, but she always came back. It began to happen more often and when I tried to find out what was going on with her, our conversations led to arguments. I was beginning to wonder if she was having an affair or secretly on drugs, but I found out that she simply couldn't control her anger. One day, after an unusually rough night of arguing, she got drunk and tried to stab me."

"She did?"

"Tried. I'd never seen her that drunk before. She just went ballistic. Before I knew it, she disappeared into the kitchen and came back with a carving knife. She came out swinging it and trying to slash me. I eventually subdued her, but I could see the intent in her eyes. I made her leave that night. I was so shocked I could barely think. And the next morning, I woke up totally devastated. I knew that no matter what she said or did after that, I'd never be able to trust her."

"Oh, my God."

"When I was little…" Sandrine paused for a long moment. It seemed that she was debating the direction her thoughts were taking her.

She began again. "When I was little, my mother abused me emotionally and physically. My father didn't know about most of it because she always waited until he was at work or out of town. I never knew when the yelling or the beatings would come.

"Years later, when I was with Chris, I told my father about my mother. I thought he would die. He was totally distraught. I felt even worse telling him because of the pain I caused him. But he encouraged me to seek counseling. He even went with me to many sessions. I was just beginning to understand that in the isolation of my own mind, I was forming some very cynical perceptions of people. I was working on realizing that not all people would hurt me like my mother did. And then the incident with Chris happened."

Sandrine looked hesitant, as if she thought she might be revealing too much. Laney put her hand on Sandrine's knee and squeezed it, and Sandrine seemed to gather her nerve.

"After Chris attacked me, I began to have nightmares. In my last session with the counselor, we talked about the connection between Chris's behavior and my mother's abuse. And that was as far as I could go with the therapy. All I could think about were Chris's eyes. Her expression was the same as my mother's during the times she yelled at me or hit me."

Sandrine dropped her head and gazed into her lap. When she had been silent for a few moments, Laney took her hand. "That was a lot to go through, Sandrine."

"I let my fear take over and quit therapy."

"We can only handle so much. You went as far as you could at the time. There's no shame in that."

Sandrine looked up, her smile tight-lipped. "After my first date with you, I wished I had gone further." Her eyes fluttered for a moment. "I still feel broken."

Laney's chest felt heavy and her heart ached from hearing what Sandrine had gone through. "Well, I think you're doing great."

"You're too kind."

"And you're incredible."

They stayed in Laney's car and talked a while longer. There was something very special about this woman, and Laney's attraction for her was growing quickly. Sandrine was courageous and resilient.

She made her feel comfortable, and Laney respected her quiet confidence, her gentle spirit, and especially her attentive demeanor.

After a while, Sandrine covered her watch with her hand and said, "I don't want to know that it's past my bedtime."

"An early day for you tomorrow?"

"Yes. Very." Sandrine smiled. "And I'll think of this date all day." Uncovering her watch, she stroked Laney's cheek lightly. "You're a breathtaking woman, Laney."

Sandrine leaned over and they kissed, Sandrine's lips caressing Laney's softly. When her lips parted, Laney met her tongue in a slow, easy dance. Laney melted as Sandrine's warm hand stroked her face. She felt her sweet breath and the tickle of her hair brushing her face. The kiss felt better than any she'd ever remembered feeling.

On her way home, Laney realized how much she had enjoyed the simple and real pleasures of the evening. She would rather merely kiss Sandrine than do anything else with another woman.

In contrast, things were getting old with Theresa. The sex had been fun, but their relationship had nowhere to go. Maybe she wasn't cut out to play the field or have unreserved sex without much emotion. Sure, the lust and excitement were there with Theresa. Laney's body immediately reacted to her touches, her breathing accelerated, and she instantly got wet. But her mind almost went blank. Laney's arousal was simply a reaction to the performance of her body parts. Theresa would probably hold her if Laney asked, but she wouldn't do much more than that. Theresa would go back to her husband and, other than some conversation on the phone, usually to tell Laney about the next outing of the Pleasure Set, they would have no real contact.

Obviously they had established that dynamic between them: straightforward sex. And while it was certainly satisfying, the satisfaction was totally corporeal. Theresa definitely knew what to touch and kiss and how to move her body against Laney's, but they didn't share any joy, ardor, or true, deeply felt passion.

However, time with Sandrine was wonderful and stimulating.

And they had a deepening connection that Laney wanted to foster and grow.

She pulled into her driveway and killed her car's engine. A revelation surfaced, extraordinary and concise. She had been experiencing two different people in two different ways. With Theresa, her feelings were concentrated between her legs. With Sandrine, her feelings lived in her heart. There it was, right there. That was the difference between sex and romance. And romance felt better.

CHAPTER FIFTEEN

Sandrine awoke to the sun shining in her window. Normally, she was up before dawn, but she had luxuriated in sleeping in and now lay there smiling.

Dinner the night before had been fantastic. She could hardly comprehend that she had actually had a second date with Laney. The thought reminded her of classic black-and-white movies where the main characters pine over one another and both of them struggle through most of the movie until they can finally fall into each other's arms.

Her longing for Laney through the years of their business relationship had been like a yearning from afar. But now it seemed they had reached the falling-into-each-other's-arms part.

She had begun to mentally sift through her compulsory errands for the day when her cell phone rang.

"Hello?"

"Good morning." It was Laney. "How did you sleep?"

"Very well. And I hate to admit it, but I haven't left my bed yet."

"Ah, it's a lazy Saturday morning, is it?"

"Very much so." Sandrine couldn't imagine a better voice to hear first thing.

"I called to ask a favor."

"Sure, Laney, what is it?"

"Unlock your front door."

"Unlock my…are you here?"

"Yes. I hope that's okay."

Sandrine jumped out of bed and headed for the door. "Well, that depends."

"On what?"

She opened the front door and lowered the phone from her ear. "Whether you can stay for a while or not." Laney, wearing a pair of beige shorts and a yellow T-shirt, looked incredible.

"A while," Laney said as she hung up her phone and stepped in. When she glanced down at Sandrine's boxer shorts and flimsy BHPD T-shirt, her eyelids fluttered slightly, which Sandrine hoped was a good thing.

Closing the door, she took Laney by the hand and led her to the kitchen. "Coffee?"

"Perfect."

When two hot mugs of java rested in front of them at her kitchen table, Sandrine suddenly laughed.

"What's so funny?"

"I just realized that I should be a lot more bashful about my appearance, but I feel very comfortable."

"Don't change on my account. I'm the one intruding on your morning. And besides, you look fantastic."

"Not too butch in these boxers?"

"You couldn't look butch if you tried." Laney added quickly, "Well, not unless you wanted to look butch."

"I don't know how I look, but as long as you're okay with it, I don't care what it's called."

Laney kissed her. "Don't change a thing. As a matter of fact, next time we go out to dinner, I'd like you to wear this outfit."

They both laughed and Sandrine pulled her into a longer kiss, which tasted of newly roasted coffee. Laney moaned when Sandrine drew away.

"Bring your mug," she said, and led Laney to her bedroom. She placed her mug on the nightstand and nodded for Laney to do the same. "Take your shoes off," Sandrine instructed, crawling into bed.

Laney didn't say anything. When she took off her shoes and straightened her T-shirt and shorts, she seemed almost self-conscious. She joined her in bed and Sandrine put her arm around her. They lay face up, not speaking for a few minutes. The sun warmed the comforter, and the sounds of blue jays mingled with the clipped squawks of a few fox squirrels scurrying in the trees right outside the window.

"Thank you for listening to me last night."

"Thank you for sharing that with me. I want to know about your life."

"All the bad parts with the good?"

"Yes."

"Well, here's a good part. It feels good to have my arm around you."

"It sure does." Laney snuggled closer to Sandrine's shoulder. "You get a lot of sunlight in your room."

"I'm very lucky to have gotten this house."

"How long have you had it?"

"I bought it right after making detective. My father helped me, but I've already been able to pay him back."

Their conversation fell into a comfortable silence and Sandrine was truly happy.

"I'm really glad you asked me out, Sandrine."

"I am, too. I had been thinking about you for a long time. Not that I ever wished for you to break up with Judith, but I always hoped that one day I'd have the chance to approach you. I hope it wasn't too soon, but I really wanted to know if you would go out with me."

"It's wiser to find out than suppose," Laney said.

"Hey! That's another Mark Twain quote."

"Well, based on our dinner conversation, I figured you could relate to another one."

"It's adorable that you love Twain, too."

"So will it alarm you that, humanitarian ideals aside, my real connection came from reading *Tom Sawyer* and realizing that the book reinforced my identity as a pretty serious tomboy?"

Sandrine chuckled, turning her head toward Laney. "As long as you're okay with the fact that I had a huge crush on Becky Thatcher."

With Laney's head now turned toward her and their noses less than three inches apart, Sandrine was suddenly electrified. "And, by the way, it was wiser to find out about you than to suppose."

"What have you discovered so far?"

"That you're agreeable to having dinner with me. That you like me a little, I think."

"True on both counts."

"Also, that if I were to kiss you, you would probably reciprocate."

"True again."

Sandrine moved onto her side. Laney followed suit and now they lay face-to-face on the bed. Laney wrapped her arm around Sandrine, and they kissed and nuzzled each other's necks, learning every detail of the other's face, mouth, and neck. They moved at a slow, lingering pace, and only after a long while, when their breathing gradually began to increase, was there any indication that things were progressing.

Laney's hand moved down to stroke Sandrine's thigh, massaging and kneading her quadriceps in gradually widening circles.

Sandrine marveled at this new experience. In the years she had known Laney, she had at times allowed herself to fantasize about what her body would feel like. How would she move? How would her body feel when she was aroused? A thrill of pleasure and anticipation raced up her spine. The benevolent Goddess of Fate was delivering the answers to these questions.

Sandrine moved her hand down Laney's shoulder and over her chest. Tenderly, she caressed her breast through the yellow T-shirt and Laney murmured something she couldn't understand. She drew unhurried circles around Laney, but the touch sped up her own heartbeat. She was completely mesmerized so she didn't notice that Laney's hand had also begun to roam from her thigh and downward until she felt her massaging her backside. Laney's hand felt cool through the thin fabric of her boxers as she gently squeezed her cheek. Sandrine pushed her hips into Laney, who responded with a moan. Sandrine savored the soothing onset of pleasure and her sense of elation.

"This is amazing," Laney said as she nuzzled Sandrine's neck.

"We fit well together."

"And more than that. The feelings inside…" She paused, seeming to collect her thoughts. "I feel so much more emotion with you than I have in a long time. I really, really like you. I feel it in my chest. Does that sound silly to say so soon?"

"Not if you feel it."

"I do."

"I know what you mean. Being with you makes me forget everything else. And everyone else."

They continued kissing, and when Laney slipped a single finger under the boxers, Sandrine's breath caught in her chest. Laney held still for a long while, then eased past Sandrine's small patch of hair. Sandrine held her breath until she felt the slick, wet slide of Laney's finger over her clit. Then her body involuntarily constricted.

They stayed in this magnificent moment a long time, Laney lightly stroking her while Sandrine massaged her breast. Sandrine felt drunk, overcome by the infatuation she had harbored for so long for the woman who was now touching the most private part of her body.

She wanted more but interrupted their kissing to say, "You feel incredible, Laney. But I do want to take this slowly."

"I do, too. But I'm not sure I can stop."

Sandrine could focus only on the blue eyes that burned with ardor. She shook her head, realizing that her last sentence wasn't the truth. "I don't want you to stop."

"But I will if you want," Laney whispered, her expression smoldering.

Sandrine believed Laney, which made her want more. And as her need began to slam a rhythm in her chest, she said, "Just a little bit more."

Laney looked hard into Sandrine's eyes, as if asking whether she really meant it, as if making sure she had permission.

Now Sandrine couldn't stop if she wanted to. "Maybe more than just a little." She closed her eyes, feeling their shared heat. Their skin seemed to meld together, exchanging sexual energy and passion all the way down to the cellular level. She wanted it all. She wanted Laney and nothing else. And as she gripped Laney tighter, Sandrine felt two of Laney's fingers slide inside her. Like a shot of whiskey rushing straight to her brain, the rush of Laney's penetration cascaded thorough her body.

She left Laney's breast and threw her arm around her back, clutching her tight. Laney kept her fingers just inside, never plunging or speeding up, but moving carefully, with excruciating deliberateness.

"Oh, God," she moaned.

Laney buried her head in Sandrine's neck. "This is amazing, feeling you like this."

"Just stay right there."

"I will."

It was such a subtle movement, Laney's fingers barely inside her, but Sandrine's muscles began to tighten. Part of her wanted to stop, to slow down so they could build a relationship without jumping into the physical aspect that sometimes bogged down true communication and understanding. She didn't want this to be like some of her other liaisons, where the pleasures of the flesh dominated and sometimes ruined things.

But lying here with Laney was already better than the most intimate of her experiences. She let go, shutting out her thoughts, and concentrated on the intimate connection they were making right then. That was the best way to let Laney know how deeply she felt about her.

As she gave herself to Laney, her entire body grew hot. Her thighs shook and her clit swelled as a fiery surge rose from deep inside and created multiple contractions. She cried out, grasping Laney's shirt, her hips thrusting up to meet Laney's gentle fingers. Her body pulsed against Laney. Sandrine was taking her to the deepest place inside her, and it felt right to go there with Laney.

Afterward, they lay motionless. Sandrine finally slowed her

breathing and, after one substantial and satisfying sigh, opened her eyes. "Wow."

Laney slipped an arm underneath Sandrine and pulled her close. "I adore you," she said, and they cuddled together, peaceful and relaxed, until they both drifted off to sleep.

Some time later, as they both began to awaken, Sandrine smiled when a light kiss touched her lips.

"Hi."

"Hi." Sandrine kissed her.

"I want to know more about who Sandrine Girard is."

Sandrine inhaled a breath full of fresh morning air, satisfied and peaceful. "What do you want to know?"

Laney smiled as if she were about to be granted a wish from a genie. "What's your favorite food?"

"A grilled-cheese-and-bacon sandwich."

"Okay, what's the first thing you'd do with a million dollars?"

"Pay off this house."

"Smart. I like that in a woman. Another question. If you couldn't be a crime fighter, what would you do for a living?"

"Hmm. I would be a stripper."

"Really?"

"Yes. I like the feel of antique wood and the smell of orange oil polish."

Laney pinched Sandrine's shoulder. "A furniture stripper, funny."

They laughed together and when they fell into a comfortable silence, Sandrine took Laney's hand and languidly played with her fingers.

"That feels good," Laney said. "Let's see. I know, what's your biggest regret?"

Sandrine closed her eyes. She could come up with a number of responses, all true, but none that could come close to her biggest repentance. As much as she wanted to dodge the real answer, she had to start to change. Her life had been miserable for so many years. Maybe this was her chance for absolution. She turned to Laney, beautiful Laney. "Hesitation."

Sandrine knew the answer was ambiguous and that she needed to elaborate. She had opened a door that she didn't want to close. And it seemed Laney sensed her unease, because she took her hand and tenderly kissed her knuckles.

"Three years ago, I was with another detective at the house of two suspects." Sandrine was uncertain whether she could even recount the events that she had refused to talk about after the investigation ended. "We had a search warrant and rang the doorbell. We heard some scuffling on the other side of the door, and in a flash, shots were fired and the bullets came through the door. Tom and I jumped away, each in a different direction, and somehow avoided getting hit.

"We both fired a few rounds at the house to hold them off. In the midst of it, he yelled, 'Come on, we have to get out of here,' but I argued that we had to stand our ground and call for backup. I also yelled back that they would shoot us in the open space we had to run through to get back to the car. He said he would cover me while I ran, and I remember shaking my head. Then he said, 'Come on, trust me.' He thought I would take off running at that moment, but I hesitated." Sandrine's throat tightened and she began to cry. Laney took her hand, rubbing it gently, but she could barely feel the motion through her shame.

"He came up from his crouch and when I saw that, I began to run. But I was a second too late. They shot him before he could cover me."

Laney's eyes were open wide but, thankfully, she didn't interrupt. Sandrine wasn't sure she could continue her painful confession if she had to pause again.

"He went down and I began shooting into the house while I made my way over to him. He had been shot in the shoulder so I grabbed his other arm and dragged him to the side of the house and radioed for help. It wasn't good cover. They could have shot from the side window at any moment, but that was the only place I could get him to fast. I called for backup and we sat there for maybe five minutes. Nothing came from the house but silence. When SWAT arrived they were able to pull the ARV, that's their armored rescue vehicle, up to us and get us in. They eventually raided the house and apprehended the suspects. Tom was in the emergency room for four hours and I stayed right outside until he was moved to a room."

Sandrine looked deeply into Laney's eyes, wondering if she could understand the gravity of the potentially deadly mistake she had made. But all she saw was loving concern.

"I had to see him. To apologize to him."

"You saved his life, Sandrine," she said softly.

"I almost got him killed."

"Even if you had run a second sooner, they still could have shot him."

The police department's Internal Affairs investigation reached the same conclusion. She had been cleared of any wrongdoing, and Tom had failed to see any foul-up on her part and had even thanked her for saving him, but she knew in her heart that her moment of distrust had spilled blood.

"My biggest regret was hesitating. But trust. That's the real problem. And that's my fear. As soon as he said 'Trust me,' I froze." She wanted to tell Laney more about her mother and her nightmares but she was suddenly exhausted. As her tears spilled freely, she also couldn't tell Laney that the incident had destroyed her professional self-confidence for the next year.

Laney wrapped her arms tight around Sandrine. A lawn mower began to sound in the distance, and a basketball bounced a couple of houses away.

Laney kissed her forehead. "I want to get to know you so much more."

Sandrine struggled to suppress the feeling that she didn't deserve happiness for her awful deeds. But if her father could love her unconditionally, others might do so, too. She had to believe in that possibility with all her heart. She took a deep breath and released it slowly. "Yes. I'd like that." She smiled, feeling a little less lost. "As a matter of fact, I really want to get to know you better as well so I won't think of you as a longtime fantasy, but a wonderful reality."

Laney sat up and reached into her pocket. Sandrine rolled onto her side, watching her. After pulling something out she lay back down on her side, facing Sandrine.

"See this?" Laney showed her the keychain that held her keys. On it was an old quarter with a hole drilled through it. "This was the first payment I ever received at the bank. When I was about eight, I went to the bank every day and cleaned up the teller areas, stacked withdrawal and deposit slips, replaced dried-out pens, things like that. My father paid me twenty-five cents an hour. It meant a lot to me to work for my father. I always dreamed of having a career there when I grew up." She looked down at the coin. "Anyway, my father helped me drill the hole and I wore this quarter on a chain around my neck for years. I feel proud every time I look at it because from that first day, I wanted to help make the bank the best in the world. I dreamt of running the bank one day."

"That's wonderful," Sandrine said, watching Laney finger the coin lovingly.

Laney took it off the ring and handed it to her. "My dream came true. I am working in my family's business, and I'm very proud of that accomplishment. Now I'd like to give this to you."

Sandrine shook her head. "No, I couldn't accept it."

"Please do. It's for you to keep. That way, I'll become more than just a dream to you."

Sandrine closed her hand over the quarter, touched deeply. "I'll always protect this."

"I know you will." Laney kissed her sweetly.

❖

Laney had been missing so much work, coming in late or being exhausted while she was there, that she went straight from Sandrine's house to the bank to catch up. Since it was already late Saturday afternoon, the place was empty, so she could focus on her paperwork and do the weekly reports. More than that, she wanted some quiet time to reflect on her morning with Sandrine.

She hadn't expected all that happened. She had decided to stop by because she had been thinking about Sandrine so much.

She wanted to say hello and talk for a while—just be around her. She wanted to be close to her and kiss her but was also willing to go wherever Sandrine wanted to take her. And where they went was lovely. The morning had turned out better than she could have imagined. Feeling Sandrine's body and the way it responded to her had been mind-blowing. But when Sandrine had shared, with such candor, the incident with her police partner, Laney had been so moved that she wanted to protect Sandrine from all the world's evils.

To have both a powerful physical desire and an intense emotional affection for her was sublime. And to have the desire and affection returned was astounding. Everyone else fell away in her mind, especially Theresa, who gave Laney only mechanical sex.

Sandrine was more of a woman than anyone she had ever met. Laney felt warm tenderness and longing when she was with her. And everything seemed perfect when they were together.

Sandrine. Yes, I could fall in love with her.

Laney was glad she was the only one in the bank because her extreme happiness was obvious. She couldn't concentrate on any work for at least a half an hour because her body vibrated with the memory of being so close to Sandrine. She understood the importance of such an opportunity to explore a relationship with an amazing, brilliant, confident, and beautiful woman.

She sipped her coffee. The java had grown lukewarm but it tasted great. She wrapped her hands around her mug, feeling its cool ceramic smoothness.

Okay, DeGraff, get your mind on your work.

As president, she was responsible for overseeing asset and liability management, strategic planning, budgets, and investment strategies, as well as deposit operations, and security and facilities management. She was a day late in running the internal SAR for the last week, so she called it up on her computer. The Suspicious Activities Report would flush out any problems or dubious transactions that occurred during regular banking hours.

As she reviewed the computer-generated list, she languidly tapped her pen on the desk. Kay's name was on the list, as she had deposited nine thousand dollars when Laney opened the account for her. Because her bank, like any other, would have to report any deposited amounts of ten thousand dollars or more, the list was designed to spit out any amount just under that in order to expose potentially illicit activities. Kay had said she wanted to be careful about her deposit, so when that amount had signaled the computer to kick out Kay's name, Laney wasn't surprised.

What did surprise Laney was that Theresa must have been in the bank the day before, because there was a deposit for nine thousand dollars into her account. Why hadn't Theresa stopped in to say hello? Laney had been there all day. Kelly had brought lunch in, so Theresa couldn't have missed her.

Laney scanned the list and suddenly sat upright. Not only Theresa and Kay, but Morgan Donnelly and three other women from the Pleasure Set had all made deposits into different accounts. And the amounts were all the same. Nine thousand dollars. They were all depositing identical sums just under the government's red-flag amount.

A frightening realization reverberated inside Laney's head. Like all bank presidents, Laney was more than aware that the Bank Secrecy Act of 1970, which required that all transactions in excess of ten thousand dollars be reported, was intended to curtail one very out-of-control crime. Money laundering.

Laney felt so faint that she dropped the paper. "Oh, shit."

CHAPTER SIXTEEN

Laney spent the weekend in a state of shock. She wouldn't answer her phone. She threw her mail across the room. She pounded her fist on the kitchen counter. She swore out loud, screaming at Theresa and the whole fucking mess. As she paced around her house, she grew even angrier.

How could they do that to my bank? Who the hell do they think they are?

She wanted to call her father, but the bank was her responsibility now. How could she explain to him that she had somehow allowed this to occur? He had built the bank with such care and conscientiousness that all his trust and confidence in her might dissolve if he discovered her connection with the women involved in this scheme.

She had to take care of this situation herself. And she definitely could. She had dealt with many bank crimes—fraud, kiting, and more illegal wire transfers and check deposits than she could count. And for almost every case, she had worked with Sandrine to flush out the criminals and bring them to justice.

Sandrine. *Shit!* She would have to include Sandrine.

Or would she?

❖

Though Laney hadn't slept much the entire weekend, she finally gave up all hope of rest and was in her office at five Monday morning.

When Kelly arrived three hours later, she surveyed the mounds of paperwork and empty coffee cups on Laney's desk. "What the hell?"

Laney looked up. "Just a lot of work to do." And while that was true, what she was doing was much more serious than business development and strategic planning.

She had spent hours going over recent wire-transfer records, trying to identify any unusual activity in the accounts of the women in the Pleasure Set. She had also checked the monetary instrument records for possible currency structuring that would isolate any illegal fund activity. Finally, she pored over the velocity-of-funds report that highlighted total debits and credits flowing through the women's accounts. She needed to see if a pattern of laundering emerged.

She had to find out what the entire scheme looked like. Hours of printouts and cross-referencing made her eyes blur, but terror hammered in her heart as the conspiracy began to materialize before her.

The Pleasure Set had wasted no time setting up operations at her bank. While they had been at it for just shy of three weeks, the money laundering was careening through her bank at full tilt.

And what she uncovered just before the bank opened for business that day made her sit back in astonishment. *Goddamn them,* she spat, anger seething in every pore. The trail of money led into and out of the Morgan Art Gallery—the same place many people had seen her just a few nights before.

❖

All day Tuesday and Wednesday, Laney avoided everyone and everything but work. Theresa had left quite a few messages that went unreturned. The Pleasure Set had gone to Equinox on Saturday night and had met at the Tire Store on Sunday. Theresa had called about wanting to get together Monday, as well, but she hadn't mentioned where. Laney worried continually that Theresa would come by the bank to see her. And she was also fuming. She didn't know what to say or do yet, and she needed time to come up with a plan. She had spoken with Sandrine a few times, and while their conversations were terrific, she was holding most of herself back. The truth of what was happening at the bank clawed at her stomach and tainted everything she did.

Every time she thought of telling Sandrine, she concluded that she needed to try to solve this problem without involving anyone else. She needed to confront Theresa and tell her to clear all the accounts out of her goddamn bank. She had no idea how Theresa would react and, quite frankly, she was a little afraid. Theresa was powerful, backed not only by many influential people but a lot of money.

But to avoid having the bank be the victim of this crime and to rectify what she had unintentionally caused, Laney had to deal with Theresa. *How dare she come in and fuck with my business?*

Laney had girded herself for the phone call to Theresa, and as her heart pounded in her ears and her hands shook as she held the receiver, the phone went to voice mail.

She left a message telling Theresa to meet her that evening at the bar in the Bonaventure Hotel in downtown Los Angeles. She was fairly certain that the paparazzi wouldn't be hanging out there. She couldn't risk any more photos of them together.

❖

Theresa walked into the Bonaventure bar wearing expensive black slacks and a lavender top that made her tanned skin glow. She found Laney immediately at the booth Laney had picked in the farthest corner.

"You look gorgeous, Laney." Theresa kissed Laney's cheek before she took a seat.

Under the table, Laney balled her hands into fists. She needed to stay focused.

As soon as drinks were served, Theresa said, "What's wrong, Laney?"

"A lot of things. Your bank account, for one."

"My account? What's the trouble?"

"I don't think I need to talk out loud about it in a public place. It's the same thing that's wrong with Kay Kitterman's and Morgan Donnelly's. Not to mention at least three others I've found."

Theresa stared at her a moment, then sighed. "Laney. I've explained this to you before. Those women are in the same predicament I'm in. We need to have money that's ours, separate from our husbands'. They can, and usually do, leave us at any moment, without a cent. No one needs to know about the accounts. They're not hurting anyone."

Laney took a deep breath. "It's not about hiding money from your husbands. It's about hiding it from the government."

"The government? What do you mean?" Theresa looked confused.

Had Laney gotten this all wrong? Was it just a matter of stashing money from spouses? She shook her head. No, it wasn't. The paperwork told an irrefutable story. "You have money going in and out of the Morgan Art Gallery and then in and out of your accounts. I don't have access to the records of the gallery, but I can tell you that there will be sales recorded of illegal means and gains."

"Means and gains? You sound like a statistician."

"I sound like a bank president who has found a," she lowered her voice, "money-laundering scheme. In my bank, goddamn it."

"Laney, we're all part owners in Morgan's business. We sell artwork, mostly on consignment. And we also buy artwork. Money in, money out. It's a sort of hobby for us."

It was possible, Laney thought. Theresa did sound convincing. And this was the woman she had let get close enough recently to have sex with. More than once. And in wild ways. Her original objective began to waver a bit. Granted, her new friend and this exciting group of women were certainly in a different league. Though Laney wasn't the type to buy and sell expensive art, that's exactly what some people did. Maybe it was just a rich woman's version of baseball card trading.

But no, damn it. She smelled the stench of money laundering.

She was a goddamned trained professional and knew a crime when it reared its illicit head.

She took a deep breath. "If that's all it is, you shouldn't care that I need to report the deposits and transfers to the government."

Theresa stared at her in silence. And then her next words were measured and remote. "Why would you do that?" Theresa's entire demeanor was suddenly dead calm. Too calm, actually, which frightened Laney.

"First of all, I'm bound by law to report any deposits or transfers over ten thousand dollars."

Theresa jumped in quickly, "None of our deposits...none of my deposits, I mean, are over ten thousand. You're not bound by law to do anything."

"You're right. However, second of all, I'm bound by my position as the president of the bank to report suspicious activity. And I consider multiple deposits and transfers just under the reportable amount suspicious."

Theresa placed her hand over Laney's. "Please don't do that, Laney. We're just trying to fuck those who would fuck us first. Do you know what I mean?"

Laney slowly pulled her hand away. "It's more than that, Theresa."

"It's a way to make income without our husbands getting control of the money. Don't you understand?"

"What I understand is that the paper trail tells another story."

Theresa's cell phone rang and she held up a wait-a-minute finger as she answered it. She spoke a few words, then covered the phone with her hand. "I've got to take this," she said as she stood up. "Please don't do anything until we can discuss this more. I've got to run. Thank you for the drink. We need to talk soon." She kissed Laney's cheek and was gone.

Laney sat in the booth until her heartbeat slowed. The issue was not the least bit resolved, as she had wanted it to be. But no matter what else Theresa planned to say to her, Laney wouldn't back down.

❖

"Laney." Kelly was standing right in front of her desk, which she usually didn't do. Normally, she called out from her desk or stood at her door. And her apprehensive expression surprised Laney.

"Yes?"

"The police are here to see you."

"Detective Girard?"

"No," Kelly said quickly, then lowered her voice. "Homicide."

"What?" Bad news of a death of a loved one raced swiftly through her mind. *Who is it? A family member? A bank employee?* "Let them in."

"Ms. DeGraff, I'm Detective Bruce MacRae and this is Detective Jack Townsend from Beverly Hills PD." The taller of the two men opened the lapel of his jacket to flash his Beverly Hills detective badge, its oval shape bearing a sunburst behind the city hall building and the black cloisonné ribbon that read Beverly Hills Police. She knew the badge well, having seen it on Sandrine many times.

"Please sit down."

Detective MacRae handed her his business card and she took it without looking at it.

MacRae continued. "We're here investigating the murder of Candace Dooring."

It took a minute for the words to register. "Candace? Oh, my God." Her mind spun in confusion. *Candace is dead?* Laney had just been with her at the art gallery Thursday night. *What happened to her?*

"Ms. DeGraff?"

"Yes. I'm sorry. I'm not sure what I can tell you. I hardly know her. Knew her."

From a folder he had been carrying, Detective MacRae pulled out a magazine and placed it on her desk. "This might suggest otherwise."

The latest copy of *People* magazine was open to a double-page photographic spread of celebrities at various functions. There, in the middle of them, was a photo of Candace clutching Laney's arm as they left the art gallery. The caption read: CYBER HIGH'S CANDACE DOORING LEAVES THE MORGAN ART GALLERY. Any excitement at seeing herself in *People* magazine never materialized because of the shock of looking at Candace's image and knowing she was dead.

"I've only spoken with her a few times. I got to know her a little bit for the first time that night. What happened?"

Detective Townsend said, "She was shot to death in her home the morning after that gallery event."

"Oh, my God," Laney said again. "I'll do everything I can to help you, but I'm not sure I'll be of much use."

"Do you have any idea who might have had a motive to kill her?" Detective Townsend continued.

"Like I said, we didn't know each other well. We have mutual friends and were both at the gallery function. We talked a while. We left at the same time, so when the paparazzi started crowding around to take pictures of her, she took my arm to help her get through."

"What can you tell me about the Pleasure Set?"

Laney was taken aback. "What?"

Townsend pointed to the text under the photo's caption. It read, "Candace and a fellow Pleasure Set friend enjoyed the fete for almost an hour while other Set members partied inside."

She hadn't realized that the name was known in much wider circles. Now that she was in it, what did people really know about it?

"Ms DeGraff?"

"The Pleasure Set is just a silly name given to a group of friends."

"And you and Candace are part of this group?"

"Were."

"You or Candace?"

"Both of us."

Detective MacRae took over the questioning. "And where did you two go afterward?"

"Nowhere. She got in her car and left and I walked back to mine."

"So that's the last you saw of her?"

"Yes." Laney couldn't imagine anyone killing her. "What happened?"

"We're investigating everything, Ms. DeGraff. What do you know about her?"

Laney shrugged nervously. "Just that she's an actress."

"How do you know her?"

"Like I said, through that group of friends."

"We'll need a list of names, please."

"Certainly." The photo identified her only as a friend. "How did you get my name?"

"Is there anything else you can tell us about Candace?"

Laney thought a moment. She wasn't about to reveal the times she saw Candace making out with women at the Tire Store. "I'm sorry. I didn't know her that well."

Detective MacRae picked up the magazine, then reached into his pocket and handed her a business card. "I'll call you tomorrow for the list of names. Please phone if you think of anything else that might help. We'll be in touch if something comes up on our side."

Kelly came barreling in as soon as the detectives left. "What the hell is going on?"

"An acquaintance of mine was murdered."

"Murdered? How terrible!"

"I hardly knew her."

"Are you okay, Laney?"

"Just a little shocked."

"Let me get you some coffee," Kelly said as she turned to leave the office.

Alone with her thoughts, Laney recalled Candace grabbing her arm and asking her to help get them out of the throng of paparazzi. But she remembered Candace's reticence about the group before that. She had deliberately stopped attending the private parties and started to tell Laney about it, but was cut off when Morgan Donnelly approached them.

Laney had wondered if Candace meant to warn her about the late-night walk back to her car alone, but now she knew it was more than that. And Laney had been swept up into the mess.

What the fuck is going on?

Laney squeezed her eyes shut. This was unbelievable. She couldn't comprehend the horror that Candace must experienced. An image flashed before her eyes and she shuddered as a wave of nausea roiled in her gut.

Strangely, it wasn't an image of a frightened Candace but of a steely-eyed Theresa.

Chapter Seventeen

W hat the hell am I doing?" Laney was so nervous her hands shook as she clutched the steering wheel.

Theresa had called earlier in the evening and left a message telling her of a party in the Hollywood Hills. Laney wanted nothing to do with Theresa or anyone else from the Pleasure Set. In fact, she wanted to hide in her house with the lights off until she could figure out how to get out of the mess that now threatened her bank, her family's name, and her career.

As soon as she could get her wits about her, and as soon as she could get more information about the money laundering, she would go to the police. But at present, she didn't have enough evidence to separate her from Theresa and the crime.

If she hid in her house, the situation would just grow worse. So she decided to attend the party and try to get more information. She wasn't sure how the hell she would do that but, with increasing trepidation, she realized that diving straight into the snake pit was the only way she could extract the venom.

Laney found the location of the party high up in the Hollywood Hills, on a winding stretch of dark roadway, at the end of a deadly quiet street that curved sharply upward. Parking farther up the hill, past other cars that she was sure belonged to women of the Pleasure Set, she walked down to the house.

At least forty women were in the front foyer and the living room, definitely more than she'd ever seen gathered at any Pleasure Set event. She didn't recognize most of them as she wandered through the crowd. The rooms were shadowy, similar to the ambience of most places they hung out, and Laney was thankful for the slight cover the dim lighting provided. Not seeing Theresa right away did ease Laney's nervousness, but she stayed on high alert.

Most of the women looked very drunk and no longer seemed to even notice the blaring hip-hop song that repetitively thudded out its unyielding refrain.

Laney's first instinct was to avoid Theresa for as long as possible. Theresa was too cunning to reveal any facts that would help her. She had to chat up others, women who might not know that Laney was now onto their game.

She grabbed a bottle of vodka from a counter and poured herself some liquid courage before she strode through the grand living room.

Through the murky lighting, she spotted Morgan Donnelly in a far corner, leaning seductively into another woman. Since Morgan's art gallery was the vehicle through which the laundered money ran, she wouldn't even try to get anything out of her. She had to assume that Morgan was as deeply involved as Theresa.

And just as Laney was about to turn away from Morgan's direction, she spotted Theresa through the crowd, rounding a corner and gliding into the living room.

Laney whirled around. If Theresa found her, she'd dominate her evening, leaving her unable to break away easily to pursue her mission. With her sudden change of direction, she almost walked straight into some thick, burgundy drapes that framed the wide-open doorway leading out to a deck.

Luckily, she dodged the blunder and found herself on a teak-and-stainless-steel deck overlooking the sparkling city of Hollywood below. Almost as many women crowded the deck, but they were cast in darkness, as all the outside light sconces were off.

She pushed her way toward the end of the deck so she could catch her breath and survey the party without attracting too much attention. Quickly throwing back her vodka, she resisted a cough as the searing alcohol burned her throat. Some low-slung deck chairs were lined up against the railing, and one was empty.

As she approached, a slurred voice called out to her. "Laneeeeeey!" Kay Kitterman occupied the next chair.

Laney sat down, meeting Kay halfway for a hug. "Kay, how are you?"

"Three fuckin' sheets to the wind." Kay held up a very expensive-looking and nearly empty bottle of Bruichladdich Scotch.

"I can see that."

"Didja jus' get here?"

Laney nodded and set her empty glass down on the railing. Kay could be the stoolie she was looking for. She was careful not to immediately grill Kay about the money laundering, but Kay's consciousness clock was ticking down and she would soon pass out or begin to ralph up thousand-dollar Scotch.

Laney kept an eye out for Theresa and started with some small talk as she tried to seem as casual as possible. "So, whose house is this? It's beautiful."

"Bridget Marina." It sounded more like Kay said *Bruh-jhet*.

"Which one is she?" Laney looked around at the crowd on the deck.

"She's not here."

"She's not at her own party? Why?"

Kay dispassionately took another swig of Scotch. "She's dead."

"She's dead? What happened?"

Kay put two fingers to her head and cocked her thumb up. "Pow."

"She was shot?"

"Yup."

"Was she part of our group?"

"Yeah. Sexy, too."

"So how did you all get into the house, if she's not around?"

"Theresahasa key."

"Kay," Laney had to move this along, "remember the nine thousand dollars you deposited into your account at the bank?"

Kay's eyes began to droop. She nodded.

"Did it come from Morgan's art gallery?"

"Yesss id-did."

"Did Theresa tell you to deposit it?"

"Sheee always does."

"Do you know what's going on at the gallery?"

Kay opened her eyes and focused on Laney. "D'you mean thah money hidin'?"

"Yes. How do they do it?" Laney was beginning to panic. The longer it took to get the facts, the higher the chance that Theresa would eventually find them talking and stop the conversation.

"Simple." Kay's head drooped, her chin resting on her chest.

Laney lifted Kay's chin, "Kay, how do they do it?"

Kay smiled sleepily. "Morgan makes fake art salesss an' pretendsza money comes from tha'."

"But where does the money come from?"

"Herr-in."

"What?"

Kay's eyes went glassy. "Herr-in."

Laney was so close but she was losing Kay quickly to the alcohol. Without thinking, she slapped Kay's cheek.

"Heyyyy!" Kay said.

"What's herr-in?"

Kay frowned and shook her head, this time clearly making a deliberate effort to enunciate each syllable. "Her-o-in."

A bolt of dread slammed through Laney's head. "Shit."

Kay nodded. "Guhd shit."

Laney took the bottle from Kay's careless hand. "Kay, let's ease up on the booze for a while, okay?"

"Yup. S'ok with me."

"I'm going inside now. Will you be all right here?"

Kay opened her eyes wide and blinked a few times as if trying to sober up. "Yeah. Th' freh'shair is very nice."

Clutching the bottle of Scotch, Laney shook her head as she got up from her deck chair.

"An' she was jus' like you..." Kay began to say.

"What? Who?"

"Bridget. She wuzzha bank person jus' like you." Kay giggled, finding that fact somehow funny.

Laney needed to somehow get out of the party without running into Theresa. She eased back into the living room and surveyed the crowd. She didn't see Theresa so she snaked through the women and headed toward the door.

The vodka had slightly numbed her, but her arms and hands still shook. A few women smiled at her, but she couldn't even smile back.

Kay's last comment about Bridget had confused her. She had to get out of there.

She reached the door as two women were entering. Twisting past them, she stepped out onto the porch, eyes set solidly toward the street.

"Laney."

She turned and saw Theresa holding the door open.

"Theresa." Her heart began to pound.

"Where are you going?"

"Home. I looked for you and couldn't find you so I've been out on the back deck for a while."

"Come back inside, the night is just starting."

No way in hell would she do that. Theresa's smile, which used to thrill her, now looked artificial and sinister.

"I'm not feeling well, Theresa. I'm going home." She was sure her words weren't very believable, but she was too afraid to put on any more of an act.

"Just come back in and have a drink. Or I can make you something a little easier on the stomach."

"Really, I need to go." She tried her best nonchalant smile, which felt more like a grimace. "I'll call you tomorrow." As she turned and walked toward the street, all the childhood horror movies she had ever seen rushed through her mind. She felt like a petrified eight-year-old with sharp prickles stinging the back of her neck, indicating that the monster who was right behind her, with hideously jagged talons, would, at any second, pounce on her.

Just keep walking, she told herself as she gritted her teeth, unable to breathe. *Just get to the car.*

She didn't take her next breath until she was up the street and locked into her car. She forced herself to drive calmly down the winding road toward Hollywood Boulevard. She was in big trouble, but she wasn't sure exactly how immense it was.

CHAPTER EIGHTEEN

*B*ridget was a bank vice president.
Candace was an actress.
Bridget is dead.
Candace is dead.

Laney gripped a half-full glass of bourbon as she paced back and forth through her living room.

As if the deaths weren't enough, if she could believe Kay, heroin was also involved. And Theresa and the rest of the Pleasure Set were in a dead woman's house, partying like no one cared about Bridget. Or Candace, for that matter.

It was now past three a.m. and Laney still wore her party outfit. She barely remembered the drive home, and in the hours since then she had thought about nothing but the seriousness of what her new group of friends was truly into.

How naïve was she to not see that the Pleasure Set was more than just a very private club and a wealthy networking opportunity? Was she that ignorant to believe that a bunch of seemingly intelligent, industrious, and rich women would be that clandestine without something larger behind their activities?

The rampant sex between them all certainly necessitated their stealthy behavior, but now Laney was beginning to see the bigger picture. The gravity of the situation shook her. She fell onto her couch and fought the urge to cry. The money laundering was bad enough, but she was now convinced that the deaths were part of the mess as well.

"Theresa."

Laney forced herself to remain calm as Theresa answered her cell phone. She had dialed the number thinking she might be able to extricate herself from all of this hell before it got any worse for her.

"Laney."

"I've been up all night."

"Listen, Roger's here. Why don't we talk tomorrow?"

"No. This will be short and to the point. I want you and the rest of your friends to close all of your accounts and your safety-deposit boxes."

"What's the matter, Laney?"

"You know goddamn well what the matter is. And I will have nothing to do with it. Close all your accounts and I won't report you."

"Laney, calm down. There's nothing wrong. I told you what we're all doing."

Laney began to tremble. She had to erase this mess from her bank and her life. "That line is getting old. There's illegal shit going on, and I don't want to know and I don't want it in my fucking bank. I'm dead serious."

"I can't afford to do that, Laney." Theresa's voice sounded menacing. "And neither can you."

"Neither can I?" Laney was almost paralyzed with fright, but the last comment stunned her. "What the fuck does that mean?"

"You're implicated, my dear."

"Hardly. I unknowingly facilitated your accounts and now I'm knowingly demanding their closure."

"You can't." It sounded like Theresa blew out a sarcastic snort. "You're on the tape."

"What tape?"

"Your bank's security tape. The night we partied there."

"I turned the camera off."

"And I turned it back on."

Laney's head spun as she tried to recall that night. Before she could respond, Theresa filled in the details.

"The camera was off when we went to your office. But when I went to the restroom, I switched it back on. What that means is that there is now a recording of you partying with us in the vault."

"But the camera was off when we left. I had to turn it back on."

"Remember when the wine was spilled? I went to get paper towels. I just flipped the camera back off before I came back. So, darling, there's evidence that you are more than just our friendly neighborhood banker."

A vivid memory of Laney kissing Theresa in the vault stabbed her in the stomach. She felt nauseous and swallowed, struggling not to throw up.

Theresa's voice was full of an arrogance that gave away her nastiness. And she was now angry. "Conveniently, the tape is not at your bank for anyone to accidentally see."

"You took the tape."

"I did. I simply inserted a blank one in its place."

Shit. Laney remembered an employee telling her that one of the tapes hadn't been marked. Everyone had thought that it was an oversight. Now she knew that wasn't the case.

"You're in neck deep," Theresa said, "and you will shut the fuck up and look the other way."

Once more, the monster appeared. Theresa wasn't the warm, gracious woman who had once invited her to forget her breakup with Judith and be comforted by new friends.

"You set me up, didn't you?" Laney's mind raced with a staggering new awareness. "You needed a pawn to hide your money so you wooed me with your charm and your privileged lifestyle."

And just as suddenly, Theresa's words came sickly serene and syrupy. "Calm down, honey, please. I'm truly attracted to you. I love spending time with you. I didn't think you'd be upset over hiding money from our husbands. Don't you see? They're bastards and they control our lives. This is the only way to gain some of that control back."

Theresa's transformation from angry to charming was scary.

Nevertheless, she was sticking with her bullshit story. Laney felt like she was being treated like a five-year-old. She found the anger hiding behind her fear and pulled it forward.

"I want the tape back, Theresa."

"It's a bit of insurance for me that you won't do anything stupid."

Laney didn't tell her that the tape's special formatting wouldn't allow Theresa to make extra copies, but just one original floating around could be disastrous. She fumed inside. *How dare she fuck with my family's bank?* "That's stolen property. It's marked with the bank's identification information and I want it back."

"You'll get it eventually. Just don't panic. This isn't as bad as it seems."

"And what about Candace?" She was almost yelling. "Do you think she thought it wasn't as bad as it seemed when she was getting murdered?"

Theresa lowered her voice. "What does Candace have to do with any of this?"

"You tell me."

"Nothing, darling. We're all mourning her death."

"Like you all were doing last night?"

The silence on the other end of the phone was ominous. Laney's gut lurched. She might have pushed Theresa too far. Before Theresa could respond, Laney said, "Close your accounts now." Her voice shook as she tried to regain her composure. "All of them."

"Laney, please."

Though Theresa again sweetened her words, it was all garbage.

"All of them," Laney repeated, and hung up. She wasn't convinced that Theresa would comply. And, if she was right, she had to figure out what to do next.

❖

Sunday evening slowly passed into morning as Laney spent another night unable to sleep. She had tried to watch TV, read a book, anything to get her mind off the disaster she had not only gotten into but was seemingly unable to get out of.

Finally, at six a.m. she called the bank, leaving Kelly a message that she was sick, and crawled under the covers. Burying her head in her pillow, she reviewed all her options for probably the thousandth time.

She could get a lawyer and go to the police now. They would in turn contact the Department of Treasury to launch an investigation. They would get the Financial Crimes Enforcement Network and the FDIC involved, and then it would be out of her hands while they decided whether she should be indicted in this crime.

She could tell her father, but he would insist that she go to the police and start the same process or would just do it himself.

She could simply close the bank accounts herself. The deposit agreements that they had all signed allowed the bank to do that for any reason the bank deemed suspicious. But Theresa might have new friends merely open some others. She had the original security tape to hold over her head and wouldn't hesitate to use it.

Jumbled thoughts and fragments of visuals about the Pleasure Set flitted through her brain, but no clear, concise decision or plan would materialize. After an hour, she angrily threw the covers off and took a shower.

The hot shower helped a little, but the feeling of dread had her scared shitless. Wrapped in a towel, she grabbed a diet soda in the kitchen, retrieved her cell phone from the counter, and walked back to the bathroom. She had turned her phone off, unable to talk to anyone all day, and when she turned it back on, several messages were waiting.

The first was from Hillary. Her heart sank. She'd been such a lousy friend lately. Hillary didn't approve of Theresa and had cautioned Laney to be careful about hanging out with the Pleasure Set. She certainly didn't know how accurate her warnings had been.

The next message was from Sandrine, asking if she was free that night. Sandrine said she would be home and to call her because she would love to see her.

The last message was from Theresa. Laney anxiously listened. "We'll be at the Tire Store tonight. Please come. We really need to talk. It's so not what you think. Please come."

That was the last place she'd be going tonight. Or any night.

She unwrapped the towel from around her body and let it drop to the floor. Looking in the mirror, she noticed that her body seemed oddly foreign to her. Who was she now? What had she become? What would become of her now? The alien being that stood before her was swathed in deep despair and its face was drawn long from stress.

Hillary's call had made her sad and Theresa's message filled her with shame. She had been a horrible friend and had been blind to Theresa's manipulation.

And Sandrine's message sank her into a deeper depression. She dreaded never being able to tell her what she'd let herself get into. Sandrine was a police officer, for God's sake, the last person she should talk to about this.

And she also knew what that meant. She and Sandrine were finished. Any chance for them to be lovers had been smashed into oblivion.

If she went to Sandrine, she could end up in prison, her career would probably be over, and at the very least, Sandrine would decide to have nothing to do with her.

The mirrored image before her was shaking its head in disgust. How could she have fucked this all up so horribly? She had allowed herself to be seduced into a malevolent group of women. She was mortified that she had so easily gone along with their every exploit. The lure and advantages of the elite and the benefits of celebrity had been a hollow sham. She had not recognized their façade and had let it suck her in. It sickened her that she had been a passive participant in her own downfall.

But now she was through letting others decide her fate. She had to take back control. The mirrored image stopped shaking its head. *No more*, she thought. Vowing to repudiate any further loss of control, Laney suddenly knew what to do.

CHAPTER NINETEEN

Laney was nervous waiting for Sandrine to arrive at the Change. Known for creamy coffee drinks and excellent local folk singers, the Change was a combination café and art house in West Hollywood. Normally, it would be a great date location.

She and Sandrine had just begun something wonderful. The dates had been extraordinary, and Laney had let herself wonder what could develop between them. But now she knew that what she had to tell Sandrine would kill any chance. Keeping the corruption from her wasn't an option either, unless Laney went to another detective and avoided Sandrine forever. Her heart wouldn't allow that. This evening was probably the last chance she would have to be close to Sandrine—at least for a few minutes before she destroyed what they had just begun.

Sandrine looked incredible, as usual. She walked into the Change wearing black jeans and a billowing white peasant top. A few women stared at her, which didn't surprise Laney.

They kissed when she reached Laney's table.

"It's so good to see you, Laney." Sandrine's smile sent an ache right to Laney's heart.

Laney stood. "What would you like to drink?"

"Cappuccino."

As Laney waited in line to order from the coffee counter, she grew more afraid. She dreaded ruining this night for Sandrine, but she had to at least give her the chance to end their involvement before her feelings strengthened. And maybe Sandrine would offer some advice—if she didn't throw coffee in her face and storm out, which would be appropriate.

When she returned with their coffee, Sandrine looked into Laney's eyes and seemed to study her. "Is something wrong?" she said gently.

Laney took a deep breath. "There is." She didn't know how to start. She didn't know how much to even tell her. "I'm in trouble."

"Trouble?"

"I made friends with some women and, without me knowing, they used my friendship to open accounts at my bank. I've just found out they're laundering money through those accounts."

Sandrine took this information in before responding. "But you said you're in trouble. What does that mean?"

"I did some really stupid things. This is so hard to tell you." Laney's voice caught in her throat.

Sandrine touched the top of her hand. "Just tell me what happened."

"They're a bunch of women who get together a lot. One of the things they like to do is go places at night, like places where we all work, and party. The bank was one of those places. I didn't know what they were up to at the time. I shouldn't have let them into the bank but, stupidly, I did."

Sandrine was obviously ahead of Laney. "Was the bank's security camera on?"

Laney nodded.

"And then you found out about the laundering?"

"Yes. They were making deposits just under ten thousand. When I confronted one of them, she denied it. And when I told her I planned to have them investigated, she got ugly."

"And I take it that since you're talking with me, you haven't called BHPD yet." Sandrine's voice had grown stiff and professional.

"That's right."

Sandrine hadn't yet taken one sip of her coffee, but neither had Laney. A horrible silence fell between them. She couldn't read Sandrine's face. However, she knew this was the beginning of the end for not only their relationship but for her own career. Did Sandrine's heart hold as much for her as hers did for Sandrine? If so, this confession was sure to shatter it into a million pieces. She would never get to experience and share her intense emotions. She was falling in love and wanted to give Sandrine everything, but all she could offer now was the truth.

"There's more." Laney had nothing left to lose but then noticed that Sandrine's expression had become rigid. She had totally disconnected emotionally.

"Tell me."

"They're siphoning the money through an art gallery on Melrose. I found that out when I studied the paper trail. And I believe the source of their money is heroin."

"How do you know that?"

"I questioned one of the women when she was drunk. I don't know any more than that about the heroin, but I do know the money comes through the gallery."

"This has to be officially reported, Laney."

"I know." She looked down at her coffee, crestfallen. She understood that Sandrine had shifted from lover to detective in order to protect herself. She was alone in this mess and would suffer the consequences. "There's something else." She looked up. "Two of the women from this group are dead."

"Recently?"

"One, for sure. Last week. I'm not sure when the other one died. I just heard about it. I don't want to sound paranoid, but the deaths may have something to do with the laundering scheme."

"And what involvement do you have in the heroin or the deaths?"

The words slapped Laney in the face. "None. When I started asking questions, that information came out."

Sandrine grew silent once more, slowly tapping her fingernails on her coffee mug. Finally, she said, "Laney, I want you to come down to the station tomorrow and see me. I'll arrange for a meeting with a Homicide detective as well as someone from Narcotics."

Laney nodded, humiliated beyond anything she had ever experienced.

"I need to leave now. This is a lot to take in."

"I understand, Sandrine. But I'm horribly ashamed. I didn't know what I was getting into. I'm afraid this has ruined any chance I had with you. I'm so sorry."

Sandrine didn't respond as she rose to leave.

❖

Sandrine squeezed the Glock's trigger and absorbed the powerful force of the recoil. The bullet from her service revolver pierced the human-shaped paper target right above the heart. She focused and fired another round. It hit just to the right of the last hole.

The police shooting range was fairly busy with other officers, but she blocked out their presence. She didn't know where else to go. She had just left Laney at the Change and driven down Santa Monica Boulevard, shaking uncontrollably from what she had learned. Anxiety gripped her and she couldn't sort things out. She needed some kind of release or she would explode.

She fired in rapid succession, unloading her revolver into the paper target. After reloading, she emptied the gun a second time. She fired and fired, pulverizing the target and trying to erase the shock and the doubt that threatened to destroy her trust in the one person she had started to believe in. Fifteen more rounds went into her pistol and an anguished sob caught in her throat. She coughed to suppress the rising torment and raised her weapon, firing as fast as she could force the trigger to function. With each kick of the revolver, she willed the gunshots to obliterate her reality.

Sandrine laid her revolver down on the shelf in front of her, suddenly as depleted as her gun. The ache in her heart threatened to drop her to her knees. Everything she had thought about the woman she had made love with was now in question. Laney's disclosure had shaken her faith and left her dazed.

She picked up the gun again and reloaded. Now she stared but couldn't focus on the target and she fired, barely feeling the recoil. She was aware only of her finger squeezing once, twice, three times, four.

"Girard."

A muffled voice punched through the ear protection she wore. She turned to see Bruce MacRae, dressed in Bermuda shorts and a BHPD T-shirt.

He pointed to her target. "Don't you think you need a change-out?"

She looked back down the pistol range. The target was hanging by a few strips of paper. Stunned by her living nightmare, she had been blind to what her bullets had done. It looked as if she had blown the paper human into pieces and left its severed head hanging brutalized and lifeless.

"Just letting off some steam," she said, suddenly uneasy at the obvious display of her current state of mind.

"You okay?"

No, she wasn't. "Sure."

"Bullshit."

She dropped her head and finally took a deep breath.

"It's about a woman, isn't it?"

She met his gaze. "How did you know?"

He looked around the range. "This is where I come, too."

She nodded. "It's Laney. The one I told you about."

"What's wrong? You've been so happy about her."

She let herself drop back against the shooting shelf. She should tell him what was going on. Before, she always dealt with her personal business privately, but this time, she needed to confide in someone who knew the ramifications of her situation.

"Between you and me?"

MacRae's eyes were direct and serious. "And no one else."

They collected their things and walked out to the parking lot.

With the traffic noise buffering them, she told him what she knew. It wasn't much, but MacRae comprehended the treacherous triangle that tied Sandrine to Laney and Laney to the laundering.

"It's possible that she's not guilty. Do you agree?" MacRae said after he took a moment to think about what she had said.

While MacRae waited for her response, she kicked pieces of asphalt from a hole in the pavement. With one last kick, she said, "I don't know."

"You're too young to be jaded and too old to be fooled. What does your gut say?"

"That I want to help her."

MacRae seemed to weigh the words, finding more in them than they actually stated, which was exactly how Sandrine had meant them. He nodded as if he had come to a decision. "Sometimes as cops we feel the heavy burden of living by every word that's written in the fictitious and," he tapped the side of his head, "mental edition of the good-cop handbook, you know?"

Sandrine didn't answer because she was sure there was more.

"Cops have this image of what is right. It's the black and white of it all. Sometimes, your heart gets wrapped up in the space between. And then that mental book becomes too black and white."

She had never seen Bruce look so serious and she wondered if he spoke from experience.

"Look, you'll sort things out. And if helping her means tearing out a page from that good-cop book and burning it, then know that I'll look the other way, too."

"Thank you."

"I'm certain you'd do it for me."

"I would."

He lightly shoved her arm, and as he turned for his car he said, "Now if you'd only grease that squeaky chair of yours."

As she watched him pull out of the lot and turn onto the boulevard, her throat grew tight. If she thought about the day too much longer, she would break down and never stop crying.

CHAPTER TWENTY

Laney had been in the interrogation room at the Beverly Hills Police Department with Sandrine and two male detectives for a little over two hours. A small table, four chairs, and a chalkboard were the only pieces of furniture in the room. A camera mounted in a corner of the ceiling silently watched them. How many accounts of crime and grief had these walls heard? Her story probably wasn't the worst of them, but it was certainly the worst she had ever been involved in.

She didn't have much to tell Detective Bruce MacRae, who had originally come to her with news of Candace's death. She did give the Hollywood Hills address of the house where the party took place. In her shock that night, she had only retained Bridget's first name, but the police would uncover the rest of the details.

She had even less to tell Detective Anoop Singh, from Narcotics. Laney recounted the conversation with Kay but had never heard anything else about any heroin.

Laney spent the lion's share of the time recounting the details of the laundering scheme and provided copies of the paperwork that showed the transactions. While nothing proved conclusively that money was being laundered, the indicators were there. The police would investigate the trail backward to the Morgan Art Gallery, and further back if heroin was the original source.

Though Laney felt disgraced in disclosing all these details to the police, she was mortified to have to admit them to Sandrine. And the pained look Sandrine had shown for the last two hours crushed her.

She had told them about everything to do with the bank except the security tape Theresa had taken. Certainly, they would ask to see the tapes of the days when Theresa, Kay, and others were making deposits and withdrawals, but only Sandrine knew about the tape. She was frightened to bring it up again and hoped that all the other evidence would be enough to catch the Pleasure Set. Surely Theresa wouldn't mention the tape once she was questioned.

When all the facts had been laid out and gone over two or three times, the detectives finally stood. Detective MacRae exchanged looks with Sandrine and pursed his lips slightly, but otherwise he showed no emotion. "We will call you with any other questions, Ms. DeGraff."

As Detectives MacRae and Singh left the room, Sandrine stayed, looking directly into Laney's eyes. "I don't know what to say, Laney."

Laney nodded, the predicament hanging heavily between them. But at that moment, all Laney thought about was losing Sandrine. Probably, nothing would alleviate Sandrine's disappointment, but Laney had to tell her one last thing. "Sandrine, I'm guilty of getting involved with these women and not seeing what they were planning. I'm guilty of bringing them into the bank when it was closed, something I'll probably lose my position over. But that's all. As soon as I found out what they were doing, I backed off. I'm disgusted with myself and," her throat almost closed as she choked back tears, "I'm so sorry."

Sandrine's face grew sad and she nodded silently. Looking down at the floor, she took a deep breath and left.

❖

Laney hardly noticed the usual Wednesday commerce at the bank. She had gone into work early, mostly to avoid greeting any customers. She couldn't find a smile or a happy thought and didn't want anyone to notice or ask questions.

But Kelly had noticed. She asked, but Laney made up an excuse about not feeling well, which was true. After a brutally long day, she went home and spent the rest of the evening in a daze. She needed to pick up the phone at some point and begin the necessary disclosures.

Now that she'd gone to the police, she would have to call her father within a few days and let him know what had happened. The bank wouldn't be in financial jeopardy because she had caught the crime soon enough, but her life with the bank would never be the same.

And her exhilaration and hopes for a relationship with Sandrine had been broken like a beautiful glass fishing float swept against the craggy rocks in a turbulent ocean.

Hillary would find out soon enough, but their friendship would survive. However, she wasn't sure about any other relationships in her life—business, personal, or family.

Nausea constantly churned in her stomach. And she had fallen into a depression that felt bottomless.

As the sun began to descend in the Southern California sky, Laney opened a bottle of tequila. She had forced down some buttered toast, and though she knew the alcohol would make her stomach feel worse, she didn't care. The first shot went down like gasoline. She squeezed her eyes shut, waiting for the burn that scorched her throat to subside. The second shot went down easier, and she lay down on the couch in her living room. She reclined motionless and numb until the sun dipped under the horizon, enveloping her house in murky darkness. Her mind had grown blank, which was exactly the effect she'd wanted from the tequila.

When her doorbell rang, she lay there willing the salesman or neighbor to go away. With the second ring, she got up off the couch.

Sandrine stood at the door looking neither happy nor angry. "We need to talk."

Laney led her into the living room, motioning her to the couch and turning on some lights as she did. She grew more nervous with each step. What would happen between them now? What would happen to her? Through her fright, she managed to say, "Would you like something to drink?"

Sandrine surveyed the tequila and shot glass. "How far ahead are you?"

"Two shots."

"I'll join you."

As Laney filled another glass, Sandrine said, "I'm not here to talk about us."

Laney nodded silently.

"I want to talk about the case."

Though that seemed reasonable, Laney wondered why Sandrine hadn't just called her down to the station. However, she was in no position to question her and let the thought, or any hope about them ever being together, drop away.

Sandrine summarized the conversation they'd had at the station. "So these women open an art gallery and hang up a bunch of homemade art with high prices on it. Fictitious buyers come in and purchase the art with cash, the sales are recorded, taxes are paid, and the money is clean after that."

"Yes, at least that's what it looks like."

"And you don't know who's dealing the heroin?"

Laney realized that Sandrine was allowing Laney to reveal details she might not have told the other detectives. She must have come by because sometimes people have second thoughts about holding back information.

"I truly don't know. All Kay told me was that the money came from that source. She was so drunk that was all I could get out of her."

"And you said there have been no wire transfers to overseas companies that you know of."

"Not from my bank."

"What's so odd is that this appears to be a classic type of money laundering, not contemporary."

"What does that mean?"

"In a classic laundering scheme, a business is created to ostensibly earn money, like any business that brings in a good deal of cash will do. They operate the business as usual during the day. Then they feed in the day's illicit receipts, deposit them in the bank, and spend them like everyone else does. When tax time rolls around, they pay their taxes like everyone else, as well. It all looks like a profitable business."

"Isn't that the way it works?"

"Traditionally, yes. Laundering became very popular during Prohibition. And small businesses, like coin-operated Laundromats or car-wash companies, are good vehicles. Illegal gains are made to disappear and the businesses are used to move money through because it's hard to track just how much money actually goes into the places. And then they make the money reappear in some slow but steady manner that doesn't bring it to anyone's attention."

"And how is that different from contemporary laundering?"

"Contemporary laundering uses wire transfers and other electronic means to move money around through so many different international channels that it's much more difficult to track the origin."

"So these women are just more immature in their scheme?"

"I'd say they're more old-fashioned."

"I wouldn't consider them old-fashioned. That's too innocent a description." Laney grimaced.

"Old-fashioned in that it is so simple and obvious that they thought it could fly under the radar."

"These women have it all. I doubt they really need the money. And I'm beginning to doubt that they fear their husbands are trying to screw them financially." Laney felt distraught and confused. "Why would they do this?"

Sandrine shrugged. "For kicks. To prove they can do it and get away with it. We see a lot of bored rich people do crazy things. Criminals know that we follow the money. We follow financial records. People with low-paying jobs who suddenly pull up in their driveway in a Porsche raise suspicion, and those cases are a lot easier to solve. But these women live expensive lifestyles so no one thinks twice about the money they flash.

"Your friends." Sandrine paused. "These women established

the gallery for what we call invoice scamming. They record what looks like legitimate sales, but in order to make the money reappear, they need a bank to move it to so they can write checks for other things, making everything look lawful. But they usually need someone at the bank to look the other way. Typically, that bank employee has a lucrative reason to be involved and protect the scam because they know the cash flow will stop if they don't."

"I never took money from this."

"She never offered you a cut?"

"I didn't even know about it."

"That's unusual, since the risk of exposure, due to not having anyone on the inside, is high."

Laney knew what the benefit had been. She had gained acceptance into the elite crowd. She had hobnobbed with rich, entitled women and gone to places people only dreamed of. She had been pals with actresses and made to feel like a celebrity, but not because they saw her as a friend. That stung. They had duped her into becoming a group member all because Theresa needed an ignorant foil.

That made her angry and, as she looked at Sandrine, humiliated. "I never took a penny," Laney reiterated. "And they never told me about the scheme."

"So she didn't want you to know. If you didn't know you wouldn't say no to the laundering. If ignorant about the activities, you couldn't say the wrong thing to your regulators or auditors."

"But allowing my bank to be used by someone else to launder the proceeds of a crime, even if I was unaware, can still indict me."

"Your only defense is to prove you didn't know what was happening."

"That'll be next to impossible."

"Yes, I'm sure it will."

"Have they found out anything about the deaths of Bridget and Candace?"

"They haven't debriefed me yet."

"There *is* one thing that bothers me about that."

"What's that?"

"Bridget was in the group of women, and she was the vice president of a bank."

Sandrine hardly paused before she said, "She's dead, out of the group, and now you're in the group and you're also with a bank."

Laney nodded, grateful that Sandrine was so astute.

"You were chosen to be in the group based on your position at the First Bank of Rodeo."

"Exactly."

"You were being groomed."

"Knowing that asking me to join the group was premeditated makes my skin crawl."

"I'll make sure Detective MacRae knows to investigate the possible connection between Bridget and you." Sandrine stood slowly. "Thank you for your time."

Laney flinched. Their interaction was even more businesslike than the times at her bank when they dealt with other crimes. At least before, they also chatted about their lives and had fostered a friendship. But Laney understood the severity of the bombshell she'd just dropped on Sandrine. It was the most prudent way Sandrine could conduct herself. Laney was now part of this corruption, not just the president of a victimized bank.

She walked Sandrine to the door, and when she opened it, Sandrine hesitated. Laney couldn't find words and presumed Sandrine couldn't either.

The long minute or more that they looked into each other's eyes was unbearable.

Then something miraculous happened. Sandrine cupped Laney's cheek with her hand, which was warm. Laney closed her eyes, absorbing a benevolent compassion from the touch. Was this the last tender contact she'd ever feel from Sandrine? When she opened her eyes Sandrine's image was blurred by the most recent of many tears that Laney shed.

Without another word, Sandrine kissed Laney lightly on the lips.

But Laney could tell that Sandrine was struggling. It seemed that Sandrine's desire to kiss her warred with the need to walk away. It pained Laney to know she had caused Sandrine such conflict. Laney wanted to tell her she was sorry. She wanted to tell her not to give up on them, but she made no move to do anything else.

CHAPTER TWENTY-ONE

Theresa, I got a call from the police. They want to question me about your accounts." Laney gripped the phone as she talked.

"You didn't talk to them?"

"No, one of my employees did."

"But you said you were going to the police."

"I can't. I'm on the tape, remember? Listen, I don't like what you're doing, but I don't want a scandal in my bank. I'm mad as hell at you, but it's not worth losing my job over. Anyway, it was reported before I could make the paperwork go away. I'm just giving you a heads up since I'm sure they'll call you now."

"What do you plan to tell the police?"

"Nothing. I don't know anything about it."

After a pause on the other end Theresa said, "I never wanted you to be mad at me, darling. I'll make this up to you."

Laney hung up the phone and stared at the wall of her living room. She had just taken the next step toward taking back control. She clenched her jaw, feeling its rigidity along the sides of her face. Admittedly, it had been dangerous and insane to lie to Theresa, but that was the only way she could cover herself when Theresa was brought in for questioning. That way, Theresa would believe Laney hadn't betrayed them and she would still be able to infiltrate the group and get more evidence without Theresa suspecting too much. Granted, after their last confrontation, Theresa would be suspicious of her now, but if she could make her believe she was in the same amount of trouble as Theresa, she might have a chance to clear her name.

Besides, if Theresa had been lying all along to gain the upper hand, Laney could throw one back for her own benefit.

❖

"Detective Girard." The police department front desk had called Sandrine.

"Yes?"

"You have a visitor. Front lobby."

When Sandrine reached the lobby, she looked around for the person who had requested her. She scanned from the group of people milling around asking for an officer to a couple waiting to get a yard-sale permit and spotted Laney at the far corner, looking at a glass case filled with the department's awards.

Laney turned as she reached her. "I'm sorry to bother you at work. I need to talk to you."

"Is this business or private?"

"Both, I guess."

"Let's go outside, then."

Sandrine walked Laney down the front sidewalk and to the side of the building where a patch of grass grew under two large oak trees. Though passersby strolled down the street, not many people visited the shady area except at lunchtime. They could have some privacy here.

"I didn't sleep all night," Laney said. "I can't imagine it's been much better for you. Maybe you're already on overload with everything you've found out recently, but I hope you'll hear me out."

Sandrine wanted to wrap her arms around Laney, but the urge also scared her. Everything in her told her to run from this woman she wasn't sure she could trust now.

"I know I might have messed up any possibility for us to start a relationship, but Sandrine, please believe that I'm seriously aware of my horrible choice to spend time with Theresa and her friends.

You may decide not to date someone who makes such bad choices, but that's all I'm guilty of. And as soon as I realized my mistake, I backed out of that situation."

Sandrine took the time to consider Laney's words. She could see in her eyes that she meant what she was saying, but Sandrine couldn't simply accept her explanation and forget what she had done.

Granted, Sandrine had made terrible choices in her life, a few potentially as bad as Laney's—without the legalities involved but, nevertheless, just as bad. And could she really condemn Laney based on this one incident, given the fact that she had known her a long time and always liked what she saw?

True, she had only known Laney in a business sense, but she had always trusted her ability to read people. It had gotten her far in her career. However, she had made bad relationship choices and she certainly didn't want to start the next one off on the wrong foot.

"Laney, I hear your words. But some conditions make me want to step back."

"Conditions?"

"My heart, for one. I'm pretty jumbled up. Do you understand?"

"Very much so."

"Also, you and I associate with each other on professional terms about problems with the bank. Because we're in a personal relationship, there's now the problem of ethics. Given your involvement with the perpetrators, a shadow hangs over you now and, ethically, any police officer who is, or has been, involved with someone who is embroiled in a crime is flirting with departmental action."

"I hear what you're saying." Laney's face was strained and Sandrine hurt for her.

Sandrine anxiously began to rub her forehead. "I don't know what to do."

"I understand," Laney said. "And I'll fix this."

Sandrine wasn't sure how she could at this point. At least not without going down a long, drawn-out legal road. "How?"

"I intend to get the evidence you need."

Sandrine dropped her hand from her forehead. "You what?"

"I'll get evidence to not only trap these women but to prove my innocence."

"No, Laney, you can't do that."

"I'm the only one who can."

"The risk is too high. These women could be killers, Laney."

"The risk of losing you is worse."

Sandrine opened her mouth to say more, but the impact of what Laney said hit her squarely in the chest. This woman standing before her was willing to do whatever she had to in order to clear her name and prove to Sandrine that she could be trusted. "No, Laney," she said gently, "let us handle this."

"I can get into the middle of the group, Sandrine. I can get more information. It would be easy."

"And too dangerous. Theresa already knows that you're not on her side. She knows that you don't approve of what she's doing. She won't trust you. In fact, she'll assume you're up to something and watch you like a hawk. Or worse. I can't let that happen."

Laney dropped her head.

"I wish it weren't that way, Laney, believe me."

"You do?"

"I do. I've spent a long time wanting you." There, she'd said it. "You wouldn't have known that because I'd never be obvious about it while you were with Judith. And then I had the opportunity to get to know you better, and I really liked what I learned about you and what I experienced," she took a breath, "and felt."

When Laney reached to take her hand, Sandrine allowed it but knew Laney would notice that it was shaking.

"Is there still a chance for us?" Laney said, "because I so very much want this, you and me."

"We'll have to see. I can't deny my feelings for you. But I'm being honest with you that I'm torn over this."

"I understand your feelings, Sandrine, I really do. This has threatened a deep part of you. The part your mother abused. But please don't give up on us."

Everything Sandrine wanted was standing right in front of her. *Come on, just trust this,* she tried to tell herself, but images of her mother and her partner Tom crashed through her brain. She shook her head and sucked in a shaky breath.

She pulled Laney's hand toward her. Her body followed and she kissed her quickly before she could reason the feeling away. She wrapped her arms around Laney, drawing her into a tight hug. Though the kiss had been contrary to her better judgment, it was entirely in harmony with the feelings she couldn't quite squelch.

"I'm not sure I can walk away from you, Laney. And that scares me very much. In the meantime, please listen to me and don't go see them." Sandrine's last words became firm. Then she softened her tone. "After this is over, we'll talk about us."

Laney nodded. "I'll get going now. Thank you for listening to me."

Sandrine walked back to her office with more uncertainty and longing than she had felt twenty minutes earlier. Just before she sat down at her desk, she reached into her pocket and withdrew the drilled quarter Laney had given her. She slowly flipped it over and over, studying it. The quarter represented Laney's love of the bank and her dream to make it the best bank ever. It also represented the dream a young Laney wished would come true.

What the hell should I do?

She rubbed the quarter with her thumb until it grew warm. She looked over to the pile of folders in her inbox. The First Bank of Rodeo's money-laundering case sat right on top. There, that was black and white, a group of facts and evidence. She knew how to handle that. Like all her other work, she would tackle the case with confidence and a complete command of each step along the way.

It was easy when her brain was wholly engaged. But with Laney, her heart was the driving force, and she was profoundly confused.

Why was this situation so muddled in her head? Life was usually so black and white, with either good guys or bad guys. *A* led to *B*, which led to *C*, and then the answer was obvious. It was never this murky. *My professional life is easy as long as I simply follow the facts, so why can't I resolve my dilemma with Laney?*

Why is it so hard to just walk away from her? Why isn't the answer obvious? Why...

"Oh, my God." Sandrine suddenly realized the obvious. "I'm falling in love with her."

CHAPTER TWENTY-TWO

Angry and nervous, Sandrine waited for them to bring Theresa Aguilar in for questioning. She had gone through so many mental pictures of what the woman would look like. Normally, these interviews were predictable—lots of questions and a lot of cagey answers. Many people acted as if they were completely innocent, with eyebrows and voices raised high, hoping they could convince her that they weren't guilty. Others were defensive, posturing with angry body language as if their demeanor would intimidate her enough to back off. A few crumbled at the first inquiry, crying and sobbing that they meant no harm or that horrible financial problems had driven them to the crime, expecting to be forgiven and walk off scot-free.

Which tack would Ms. Aguilar take? Sandrine felt off balance.

Just before noon, Theresa walked into the interrogation room. Sandrine was immediately stunned that she was not only attractive, but alluring, in her low-slung Prada dress and expensive jewelry. She had expected a high-class Beverly Hills wife, but this woman was all business, exceedingly gorgeous, and she reeked of charm and confidence.

Theresa strode right up to Sandrine, holding out her hand. "I'm Theresa Aguilar and you are?"

"Detective Girard. Please sit."

Sandrine opened the folder in front of her. "I don't want to keep you long, Ms. Aguilar, but I need to ask you about your association with the First Bank of Rodeo."

"Certainly." Theresa was relaxed, smiling directly at her.

"Approximately four and a half weeks ago, you opened an account as well as a safety-deposit box at the bank. Is that correct?"

"Yes, I did."

"It has come to our attention that large amounts of cash have been deposited into and withdrawn from that account. These amounts were all just under ten thousand dollars. Under the Bank Secrecy Act, these transactions have been reported and are now under investigation for fraud and money laundering."

Theresa nodded. "Yes, Laney informed me that you would be calling me about this."

Sandrine paused. "She did?"

"Of course. We're, shall we say, close. I'll tell you exactly what I told her. I've been aware for a while that my husband has been trying to divorce me. I'm also aware that he has been concealing large amounts of money so there's no evidence of it when my lawyers sue him in divorce court. The more he can hide, the less I'll get.

"So I began buying and selling art through my friend's company, an art gallery, and I don't want him to know that I'm trying to prepare myself financially for what will be a bloodbath in court. The records of these sales are at the gallery. I assure you, Detective Girard, everything is on the up-and-up." She smiled again in a charming but controlled manner.

From the moment Theresa entered, Sandrine hadn't expected her to play the scared victim or even the naïve character, but she also hadn't expected her to admit that she had deliberately hidden the money.

Sandrine made her next move. "I understand, Ms Aguilar. Nevertheless, I will forward this information to the Department of Treasury for further investigation."

Theresa sighed and leaned toward Sandrine. "I wish you wouldn't do that."

"Why is that?"

"It's Laney. I don't mean her any harm. And I'm afraid she'll get rolled up into this mess."

Where was this woman heading? "If the facts are as you say, she has nothing to worry about."

"No, it's not about the money specifically. It's just that we're together. Romantically. If that gets out during my divorce, my husband's lawyers will rake her over the coals. I don't want that for her. It'll look very bad indeed if her reputation is questioned. I mean, the bank president having sex with a married customer. You know how it is."

At the word *romantic*, Sandrine had already stopped listening. Laney was sleeping with Theresa? How long had this been going on? Why didn't she mention it? Simultaneously, shock and embarrassment stabbed her and she had to fight to keep from wincing.

"Are you all right, Detective?" Theresa stared at Sandrine with a concerned expression.

"Of course, Ms. Aguilar. However, I don't believe this has anything to do with why you're here. I'm sorry that you're having problems with your husband. But this is an investigation and it will continue."

"Am I free to go now?"

Sandrine nodded, looking down at the paperwork as if now focused on that. She couldn't trust the shock her face might reveal.

When the door clicked closed, Sandrine dropped her head in her hands trying to quell the spinning sensation that rocked her.

❖

Laney heard someone approach her office door just as the bank was closing. Looking up, she was shocked to see Theresa enter.

"I've got a surprise for you," Theresa said. "I want to make it up to you. Things have gotten a little out of hand, so I've arranged a trip."

"What does that mean?"

"Shut down your computer and come with me."

Laney had no idea what she had planned, but she didn't like any part of this offer. "Theresa, I can't go on a trip right now. I have to be at work early tomorrow."

"You'll be back in plenty of time."

"Really, I can't."

"Don't make this difficult, Laney. I truly feel horrible. We don't mean anyone any harm. And I need time to talk to you more."

"I really—"

"After tonight, I'll get the tape back to you."

If she could get the tape back and also glean some more information for Sandrine, it might be worth it. Though Sandrine had told her not to, Laney had decided to do it anyway but wanted be the one to organize the plan. And going off to some unknown locale wasn't a good one. Her gut told her to run, but as long as Theresa held the tape, she was in a position of power. Laney had to push through her fear. "Where are we going?"

Theresa smiled winningly. "You'll see."

Outside, an immense Hummer limo waited for them. The already massive vehicle had been elongated to what looked like the length of a transit bus. Sleek black windows lined the long sides, and Laney wasn't convinced it could negotiate any turns. As she got in, she discovered Kay and Morgan seated inside, champagne glasses full.

Laney turned to Theresa. "I've never seen a limo this huge."

Theresa climbed in after her. "It's a Hollywood tradition, honey." She turned to the chauffeur. "Burbank Airport."

As the limo drove away from the bank, Laney grew more alarmed. "Where are we going? I only have what I'm wearing."

"Ah, the sign of a true woman," Theresa said. "You won't need anything. It's all taken care of."

The limo was let through to the tarmac at the executive portion of the airport and pulled up next to a private jet.

As they filed out of the car and onto the plane, Theresa placed her hand on Laney's back, helping her up the stairs. "Courtesy of Morgan's husband."

In an hour, the private jet landed at McCarran Airport in Las Vegas. Another limo picked them up on the tarmac and they were at the Bellagio in less than thirty minutes.

A three-room villa awaited them and they walked in, laughing and chattering about things Laney couldn't care less about.

"We have four damn bathrooms, ladies," Kay said, "so we won't be fighting over a mirror."

"I'm taking a sauna later, anyone want to join me?" Morgan said as she surveyed the in-suite workout facility that included a massage room and dry sauna.

Laney walked through the formal dining room into a private kitchen and watched Morgan make a beeline to the fully stocked bar. Kay and Theresa stepped out onto the private terrace, which featured a garden, a pool, and a large hot tub.

How am I going to find out about the heroin? Laney scrutinized the women. The most likely candidate was Kay, since she had spilled the beans to Laney at the Hollywood Hills party. Of course, it would probably help to wait until she was drunk. But would it be that easy to get Kay alone again?

Theresa and Kay walked back inside. "All right, girls, let's hit the casino." Theresa opened her purse and pulled out large wads of one-hundred-dollar bills. She handed them out. "Bet heavy, have fun, and if we get separated, we'll meet back here in five hours."

Laney checked her watch. It was after eight o'clock. She hoped she'd have enough time to glean more information. She looked down at the thick wad of one-hundred-dollar bills she'd been given. She must have been holding at least ten thousand dollars.

Hit by the cacophony of noises when the elevator doors opened, Laney stepped out and followed Theresa and the rest. Their first stop was a craps table in the high-limit room.

Theresa and Kay immediately cashed in a few thousand and received $100 chips. As they began to play, Theresa put her arm around Laney and pulled her close. She kissed Laney's neck, and Laney was glad her head was turned away because she involuntarily closed her eyes, loathing the intimacy.

She turned her head back, smiling and wishing for the courage to get her through the evening. She forced herself to wrap her hand around Theresa's side.

"You feel good, babe," Theresa whispered in her ear. "Please forgive me. I really want to make it up to you."

Laney smiled, not sure what to say. Anything would be a lie, but which lie would be just enough to send a message of acquiescence without imparting any suggestion of desire?

"I believe you," Laney said. To make her think they were mending their friendship, she had to play along with this despicable game. She had reentered the house of malevolence and had to keep dancing just a bit longer.

"You aren't gambling. Aren't you having fun?"

No, she fucking was not having fun. She wanted to kick Theresa's ass, she wanted to see her thrown in prison on federal charges. But she had to play along with the devil incarnate. She couldn't trust her words or her voice. The less she said, the better, but she needed time to come up with something in response. Laney stepped away slightly, looking down at Theresa's chips that were stacked sideways in the craps tray. As she did so, she moved her arm from around Theresa's waist and her hand accidentally brushed her ass.

Theresa bent toward Laney's neck and murmured, "Mmmmm."

Shit, Laney thought. That was obviously a suggestion of desire, which she hadn't wanted to convey. *Fuck!*

Theresa turned to Laney. "Later, okay? For now, honey, fork it over."

"What?"

"You can't parlay anything with that sitting in your hand."

Laney followed Theresa's eyes to the cash she clutched in her other hand. She not only had to get away from a possible sexual encounter with Theresa, she also had to get away from her watchful eyes. She wanted to see what else Kay would tell her, but the actress was too busy rolling the dice that the stick man handed her.

"I don't know how to play craps," Laney lied. "I think I'll go play some slot machines." She took Morgan by the arm. "Come with me?"

"Let's go."

Laney and Morgan found the hundred-dollar machines and took seats at two side-by-side Lucky Sevens. As they fed money in, the cocktail waitress came by for drinks. They both ordered Chivas, and when the waitress quickly brought their drinks, Morgan tipped her a hundred dollars.

They talked about this and that for the first half hour. Morgan had gone through three Chivas Regals, and after Laney nervously downed her first, she took her time, sipping her second.

"How's the gallery doing?" It was time to see where she could take a conversation with Morgan.

"Doing well." Morgan stared at her machine's spinning wheels as she spoke. "Laney, we all know you talked with Theresa about the bank accounts. It's not what you think. Really. She explained to you about her divorce, didn't she?"

"Yes."

"My husband is up to the same trick."

"You just should have told me, that's all."

Morgan gulped down half her drink. "Ah. Warms the tummy. Listen, I know she should have. Maybe that would have stopped your employee from reporting it. They did report it, not you, right?"

So Theresa had probably put the rest of the women up to trying to get information out of Laney as well. She'd have to be especially careful. "That was a big mistake. I was irate when Theresa didn't clue me in."

"You know, this whole situation has many benefits."

"Like what?"

"Like this, for instance. We can go wherever we want and do whatever we want."

"This *is* nice." Laney pretended to agree. Funny, Laney thought with abhorrence, a few weeks ago, she would have wholeheartedly believed what she said.

"The company is always hot." She downed the rest of her drink and waved the waitress over again. "Whoosh. That went down smoothly. We're setting ourselves up nicely and it won't matter what our husbands do." She held up two fingers to the waitress. "Two more for each of us, please."

"No more for me, thanks," Laney told the waitress before turning back to Morgan. "But I don't have a husband."

"That you don't. There are many more benefits. How much do you party, Laney?"

"Party?"

"Yes. Weed? Pills? We can get anything very easily."

This might be her chance. "I do get high."

"So weed is your vice?" Morgan smiled mischievously.

Laney hoped she could pull this act off. She shook her head. "Crack?"

Again, she shook her head.

Morgan stopped hitting the maximum-play button. "Horse?"

"I used to. It almost got a hold of me so I stopped. But every once in a while, I"—she bobbed her head back and forth innocuously—"partake." She leaned into Morgan for effect. "Please don't tell Theresa."

"She won't care. But you don't have to tell her. Just talk to Kay."

"Why Kay?"

"Because of Rance."

The waitress returned with two drinks and left with two hundred more dollars.

"Does he use?" Laney was trying to seem enticed and prayed she didn't look stupid.

Morgan downed half of her fourth Chivas, then shook her head. "Jimmy Pick, his business agent."

"He uses?"

"Deals."

There it was. That must be the way Theresa was getting the heroin. Suddenly, the casino noise and the smoke and the lights charged her with anxiety. It couldn't be that easy, could it? Maybe she was being set up. Maybe Theresa had everyone out to con her so they could get her into more trouble or, at the very least, keep her under wraps. And if she was being set up, she might be getting in way deeper than was safe. For now, she'd change the subject and let things cool down a bit.

"I thought Kay broke up with Rance."

"She did. But they're back together. It didn't look good that they were apart. Plus it didn't help pay for our business dealings, if you know what I mean."

Actually, Laney didn't know what she meant, but before she could ask, Morgan's machine exploded with loud bells and sirens. Morgan screamed and pointed to the machine. "I just won ten thousand dollars!"

Laney laughed as a casino attendant came over to register the win. Morgan moved aside to let the attendant fuss with the machine and sat down on Laney's lap. She held up her Chivas. "Here's to a fucking good time!"

They left the slot machine, and Morgan draped an arm over Laney's shoulder as she laughed about her winnings. The odor of Morgan's alcohol-soaked breath hung in the air and mixed with Laney's palpable apprehension. Laney kept Morgan moving around the casino all evening, stopping at the nickel machines and ten-dollar blackjack tables and any other place where she thought Theresa wouldn't look for them.

❖

Finally at one a.m., Laney virtually carried Morgan back to the villa. The rest of the women returned shortly, and Laney braced for the sex party that she presumed would transpire next. Kay fell onto the couch, giggling at something her alcohol-soaked mind must have thought funny. Theresa looked at Laney and cracked a wicked smile.

"How did you do?"

"Okay," Laney said. "Morgan hit a jackpot in between hitting the Chivas."

Morgan had collapsed in an armchair and was groaning miserably. "I don't feel so good."

"Well, I wouldn't either." Theresa walked over to Laney and put her arms around her. "Morgan, you have to stop tying them on so heavily."

How could she get out of what would surely happen next? No way was she having sex with Theresa. While Theresa kissed her shoulder, she closed her eyes and concentrated on anything other than her. Anything. She heard a far-off clinking of silverware and glasses on what was probably a room service cart in the hall. Then Morgan groaned louder.

"I really don't feel good," she repeated.

Laney pushed gently away from Theresa. "She's about to throw up."

It was the excuse she needed. She helped Morgan up, and on their way to the bathroom, she gave Theresa an apologetic look. "It's my fault. I should have stopped her at three." She pulled Morgan into the bathroom, shutting the door behind them.

Holding Morgan's hair out of the way of her vomit wasn't the way Laney had intended to circumvent Theresa's sexual desires, but it was working very well. Over the dreadful retching, she heard Theresa and Kay laughing and talking loudly. Even after Morgan stopped being sick, Laney kept her there, washing her face with a cool cloth, convincing her to just sit still on the commode.

Finally, close to two a.m., Theresa knocked on the door. "We have to go, ladies. Is Morgan okay?"

Laney helped Morgan stand and they exited the bathroom. "I'm not sure she'll enjoy the plane ride back, but now's as good a time as any."

Theresa glowered at Morgan, obviously annoyed at the disruption she'd caused.

With Morgan as the obstacle Laney intended to use to keep Theresa from any shenanigans on the plane ride home, they left the villa and headed for the limo that would take them to the airport.

CHAPTER TWENTY-THREE

Sandrine started when her doorbell rang at six o'clock in the morning. Through the peephole she saw Laney standing there. The pain of longing fought with the fury that rose in her throat.

She jerked the door open. "What are you doing here?"

"Please, Sandrine, may I come in?"

It couldn't get worse, she thought. Her heart had already been stabbed when Theresa revealed their relationship or affair or whatever it was. As much as she'd thought she was okay with Laney dating others, this was just too much.

Laney entered and immediately began to chatter. She was wound up about something, but all Sandrine could make out were the words *Vegas* and *heroin* and *last night*.

"Stop," Sandrine said. "Come sit on the couch and slow down. I can't understand what you're saying."

"I found out more. I know who's dealing the heroin to Theresa."

"We don't even know yet if that's true. Kay was drunk when she told you."

"If it *is* true, I know who's dealing it."

Sandrine decided to hear Laney out and decide afterward if she should confront her about what Theresa had told her. "What do you mean?"

"Kay wanted to break up with Rance, but when we were in Las Vegas, Morgan said they didn't because it wouldn't look good. Then she told me if I wanted any heroin, to talk to Rance. Turns out, Jimmy Pick, his business agent, is the dealer. I think Theresa influenced Kay to stay with Rance because he's the heroin connection. She's been the mastermind all along. I mean, it was Theresa that got me into the group, and it was Theresa who left by herself to go to the bathroom. That's when she turned the security camera on."

As Laney continued, Sandrine grew angrier, clenching her fists to keep from interrupting her. All she could think about was that woman having her lips on Laney and her legs wrapped around her. She tried to block out an image of them together but couldn't.

"Theresa set up the whole wine-spilling thing," Laney said, "so she could leave to turn the camera off and take the tape. She's been maneuvering her way into my life all along. Choosing my bank to open her account was premeditated. She had been planning this from—"

Sandrine couldn't keep quiet any longer. "Stop," she almost yelled.

Laney shut up mid-sentence.

"We agreed that you wouldn't see them again to try to find out any more. That was stupid and dangerous."

"But I knew I could—"

"And that isn't all." Sandrine stood, shaking. "We brought Theresa Aguilar in for questioning. Why didn't you tell me you were sleeping with her?"

Laney shook her head. "We aren't anymore."

"But you were."

Laney looked down and her shoulders dropped. "We were." Gazing back up into Sandrine's eyes she said, "But we aren't now. We haven't for a while. Not since I found out what she was doing and before you and I ever—"

"That was an important fact, Laney, and you didn't tell me. What the hell else aren't you telling me?"

Laney's head fell into her hands and Sandrine waited, furious and hurt. So many thoughts ran through her head. She wanted to yell at Laney to leave. She wanted to tell her that the night they got close was all a lie. She wanted to scream at her for a betrayal she couldn't quite understand but that had burned inside her since Theresa smugly revealed their liaison.

While Sandrine angrily paced back and forth, Laney said, "I'll tell you. I'll tell you what happened. I initially began to hang out with Theresa and her friends. They had formed some sort of secret, exclusive club and invited me to be part of it. It was exciting and something I had never experienced before. Judith had just stomped my heart and I wanted to get as far away from her as possible. These women took me in and made me feel important and special. They seemed strong, like they could handle anything life threw at them. And they made themselves out to be entrepreneurs.

"At first, I was attracted to Theresa, I admit that. Then I got caught up in the celebrity of it all. But initially I couldn't see what this group was really about. Some of us went to the bank one night to have a party, before I figured out they were laundering money. I turned off the security cameras but somehow Theresa turned them back on and the tape was recorded. I didn't know she'd recorded it and taken the tape. So when I found out about the laundering, I got angry and confronted her about it.

"Now she's holding the tape over my head and has threatened to use it as proof that I knew about the laundering and was in on it from the start. But I went to you anyway because what they're doing is a crime and I can't have that happen.

"I made some horrible mistakes, and as soon as I realized what I had gotten into, I stopped seeing her and stopped hanging out with them."

Laney fell mute, tears welling up in her eyes.

Sandrine stopped in front of Laney. She wanted to charge out of her house and arrest Theresa. Maybe that way she could make all this go away so she and Laney could start over. If only she had been able to sweep Laney up as soon as Judith left, maybe Laney would have never gotten mixed up with Theresa. But none of those things were possible right now. She was involved as a police officer in this case. "She's the one you said you were dating. The married one."

"She was."

"You should have told me everything."

"Yes, I should have. I'm sorry for that." Laney stood and faced Sandrine, her eyes blazing with frustration and earnestness. "I'm culpable of falling into a group that uses sex to lure members. They brought me into the group to use me as a pawn in their scheme. You told me that. And I needed to feel special. Being with them was like a drug at first, and I took it willingly. I feel ashamed. I would never, ever take money for an illegal crime. I'm guilty of naïvely accepting the opulent benefits of celebrity. That was the price I paid for being in an exclusive club, but now I understand that the price I'll pay for letting my bank get victimized will be more severe than that."

The thought of Laney having sex with Theresa burned in Sandrine's mind, and even though she knew she should separate that from the case, she couldn't hold back. "Damn it, Laney! You had sex with her. I don't know what you were doing with me during this time. You say she was just someone to make you forget about Judith, but this has made a mess of what I thought you and I were building. All I can think about is that woman and you. That fucking criminal and you." Sandrine returned to her pacing.

"Yes, I had sex with her." Laney sat back down.

Sandrine glanced at Laney, and what she saw clutched her heart. She looked so afraid. The color had drained from her face, and her jaw muscles were clenched so tight it seemed as if they'd both hear the crack of a tooth breaking.

Laney looked up at her and said, "That's something I desperately regret. It happened before I knew what Theresa was doing. I haven't touched her since I realized there was a chance for you and me. Our times together have been a thousand times better than anything with her. I stopped everything with her because of the bank scam but, more than that, because I began to get to know you."

Sandrine couldn't talk about the emotional side anymore. It was just too painful. "I will give the information about Rance's business agent to Detective Singh in Narcotics. Beyond that, don't go after these women alone."

Laney was about to agree, then stopped short. What had she just heard? "Alone? What are you saying?"

"I don't know what I'm saying." Sandrine strode away from

her. When she reached the fireplace she gripped the hearth. "Damn it."

But she did understand what she had said. It had just come out unconsciously. She paced back and forth, grappling with her thoughts. She wanted to go after Theresa herself, but what scared her was less about the money laundering and more about defending Laney and clearing her name. She understood that Laney had an inside advantage and had even pictured Laney joining forces with her to stomp Theresa out of existence. But the thought of dragging Laney through any more of this terrified her.

Sandrine sat back down on the couch. Frustrated, she ran her hands through her hair. She stared at the carpet and changed the subject to keep her wits about her. *Stick to the facts of the case.* "Tell me about what happened at the casino."

"Other than Morgan telling me about Rance's business agent, all we did was gamble for a while."

"Were all the women gambling?"

"Yes. Theresa gave each of us ten thousand dollars to gamble with."

Sandrine looked up. "She gave you money?"

"Yes."

"How many of you were there?"

"Theresa, Morgan, Kay, and me."

"So she had at least forty thousand dollars with her?"

"At least."

"She was cleaning."

"What?"

"Cleaning the money. It's how they disappear and then reappear money—a simple casino scam. You go to a casino and buy some chips and gamble. It doesn't matter how much or what games, you just move the money from cash to chip and then back to cash. You can then go home with a story about the Vegas trip and justify the winnings on your taxes."

"I didn't know they were doing that. Shit."

"That's why I didn't want you to stay involved with them."

Laney took Sandrine's hand. Her touch felt warm and Sandrine closed her eyes. She didn't want to pull her hand away, but she also burned inside from the jumble of feelings that twisted her gut.

"I'm so sorry, Sandrine. I won't do any of that again. I'll do whatever you say."

This was the woman she had desired for so long. This was the woman she had shared dinners with and let into her most intimate place. And though Laney's eyes were swollen and red, and lines of stress and worry marred her face, all Sandrine could see were hope and possibilities from deep inside her soul.

She gave in to her yearning and kissed Laney, closing her eyes, trying to erase Theresa and the money laundering, trying to shut out what might happen tomorrow. She found Laney's tongue and connected with the woman she knew she was falling for. She felt exhilarated but helpless in her need. She longed to protect Laney but wanted to protect herself from the pain.

Sandrine kissed her harder, hoping that she could get lost in Laney and nothing else. But she couldn't. She pulled away, and when Laney reached for her, she put her hand up. "I'm sorry. Will you please go now?"

Laney rose from the couch and Sandrine closed her eyes until the door clicked shut.

CHAPTER TWENTY-FOUR

It was late afternoon in France when Sandrine called Pierre Girard, her father. She fondly pictured him drinking a black coffee and reading *Le Monde*, his favorite newspaper.

"Ça va, ma fille?" Her father's deep voice had always comforted her.

"I am well, Papa. How are you?" She cleared her throat in an attempt to keep tears of frustration and pain back.

"Je deviens vieux."

"You're not growing old, Papa." Since leaving for America, she had spoken to him mostly in English. She had grown up in a bilingual home so dual-language discussions were normal, but she had wanted to improve her English and smooth out her accent. Still, just hearing her father transported her to the childhood she sometimes wished she could escape back to. *"Tu me manques, Papa."*

"I miss you, too, honey. Tell me how you are."

She talked to him about work and then fell into the story of how she originally met Laney and about their first few dates. How excited she was to finally have a chance to get to know her. Then she described the case Laney had brought her and the difficulty she was now in.

"I have always had feelings for her, Papa. But this makes it all different. I don't know what to do. Ethically, this isn't good for me."

"Americans worry too much about what their heads say. Follow your heart, my love. You will not go wrong."

"I'm afraid to go further with my feelings. Maybe she isn't the person I thought she was."

"Don't judge this woman yet, *ma chérie*."

"This may go very badly."

"Do you believe her when she tells you she is innocent?"

"I want to."

"So you should reserve judgment until this gets resolved. You will know in the end."

"I want to, but I want to run away from this trouble, too."

"Il n'y a pas d'amour parfait."

"I know love isn't perfect, Papa."

"Ne t'inquiètes pas," he said, with all the love Sandrine knew he had for her.

She inhaled deeply. "It's hard not to worry."

❖

"My God, Laney, I had no idea," Hillary said.

Laney had shown up on Hillary's door, eyes swollen from crying and more depressed than she ever remembered. Hillary had led her to the back patio, to a quiet spot away from her lover Cheryl and their daughter Isabelle. Laney at first didn't know where to start. She had kept her best friend in the dark about all that had happened since the sexual encounter with Theresa right before her husband walked in. But all of a sudden, the tears came and then the words spilled out in rapid fire. In less than an hour, Hillary knew about the Pleasure Set, the money laundering, the murders, the heroin, and Sandrine.

"I pulled a loose thread and the whole blanket unraveled."

"Holy shit. What's going to happen now?"

"I don't know, Hill. The bank will be fine, but if this blows up any more, if Theresa uses the tape against me, I could go to prison."

"But you said you didn't know they were setting you up."

"I didn't. But that'll be pretty hard to prove."

"Have you gotten a lawyer yet?"

Laney hadn't even considered that notion. "No, not yet. I suppose I'll have to."

"Unless you can get the tape. That seems to be the only thing that could really screw you."

"Theresa won't give it to me. She said she would, but I'm sure it's just a ploy to string me along."

"What a fucking witch."

"With the broom in her court."

"And what about Sandrine?"

"She's upset, to say the least, and doesn't know what to believe. And rightly so. I told her the truth but she's pulled way back. She's on the laundering case now and I'm more involved than is ethical for her."

"But she has feelings for you?"

Tears spilled from Laney's eyes. "I don't know. Yes, she does, but they can't last through all this. Things are such a mess." She dropped her head and Hillary wrapped her arms around her and pulled her into a hug.

"Let it out, honey."

Laney closed her eyes tight, the tears burning on tender skin already raw from crying. She had never experienced such hopelessness and misery.

❖

"So, let's look at all of this together," Detective Bruce MacRae said as he sat with Sandrine and Detective Anoop Singh in a cramped office at the police station. As much as Sandrine chatted with Bruce on a regular basis, they rarely worked together. Her cases seldom included Homicide. She had even fewer dealings with Anoop, in Narcotics. But fate had brought them together with a triple shot of deception, drugs, and death.

"We've got two dead bodies. Bridget Marina and Candace Dooring were both members of this," he shuffled through his notes, "Pleasure Set group."

"Pleasure Set?" Sandrine hadn't heard the term before.

"Yeah, that's what we got from some of the people we questioned that are on the periphery. And it isn't a complimentary name. Seems they're some kind of secret, snobby club of rich women."

The name hit Sandrine in the stomach. To be in a group of women was one thing, but for it to have an actual name meant that Laney had somehow gotten involved in a group considered so objectionable and immoral that others had labeled them. Laney's participation, whatever the depth, made her nauseous.

"Anyway," Bruce said, "both deaths have been ruled murders, and both were caused by gunshot wounds and from the same caliber handgun. Let see, we also have a money-laundering scheme that's close to being confirmed. Is that right, Sandrine?"

"Yes, it is. We have all the records from the First Bank of Rodeo and will be turning this over to the Treasury Department soon."

Anoop joined the conversation. "And we have a possible heroin connection, which may be the impetus for laundering money. This laundering seems to be running through the Morgan Art Gallery on," Anoop rifled through some more notes, "Melrose Avenue. It's run by Morgan Donnelly, who's also part of this group."

"The apparent ringleader," Sandrine said, "is Theresa Aguilar. She lives in Holmby Hills."

"And Laney DeGraff is connected to this group as well." Bruce looked at Sandrine in a sympathetic way that let her know that he was uncomfortable with what he had just said, given that Sandrine had confided in him at the shooting range about her feelings for Laney.

"She is, in that she's the president of the bank," Sandrine said, "and was the one who alerted us to this crime."

"But if she's also a member of this group," Anoop said, "we can't rule her out as a suspect in the heroin dealings or the deaths."

With all her heart, Sandrine wanted to disagree, but she couldn't. "You're correct. We can't."

Bruce pulled out a magazine photo. "This photograph was taken the night before Candace Dooring's death. We questioned—"

Sandrine snatched the photo from Bruce's hand. It only took a millisecond for the information captured through the camera's lens to smash into her brain. Candace Dooring was shown outside the art gallery with her arm around Laney. Just how close to this mess was Laney, really? For a few seconds, it was impossible to hide her shock.

Anoop nudged her. "You look like you just choked on a baguette, Girard. What's up?"

Knowing her hands had begun to shake, Sandrine put the photo down. "I just hadn't seen this."

Bruce apologized and Anoop stared in confusion at both of them. Bruce eventually continued their meeting. "As I was saying, we questioned Ms. DeGraff, who wasn't able to give us much information. We're waiting for Dooring's autopsy report, since the coroner's office can't seem to roll the bodies out quick enough. We do have Bridget Marina's report. Shot with a twenty-two caliber at close range. In the head. No weapon found. No prints at the scene. No witnesses. What else do we have?"

"Well, as far as the heroin is concerned," Anoop said, "we have prior intelligence on Jimmy Pick, the business agent of the boyfriend of one of the group members. Pick has been under surveillance for six months. That info is based on another tip, but we haven't been able to gather anything useful. There's a lot of talk, but nothing concrete."

Sandrine knew where all of this was going. Laney was the best candidate to tie everything together. She had the most information and was definitely deemed a person of interest. With a sour taste rising quickly in her stomach, Sandrine knew that when someone was a person of interest, they were oftentimes just one step away from being a suspect.

"What have we found out about Candace Dooring?" Anoop picked up the magazine.

Bruce scanned his notes. "Shot in the head, same as Bridget. They're testing the evidence to see if the same weapon was used in both murders. And I'd pretty much bet on it. Anyway, Dooring was in her driveway, getting out of her car." He looked at Sandrine. "The same night that picture was taken."

This time, Sandrine steeled herself to keep her expression

neutral. But inside, she was spinning. What the hell did Laney know that she hadn't told her? How deep in this shit was she?

"And in this case as well, there wasn't a spot of evidence or any witnesses at the scene. At this point, we have to produce either the handgun or a confession."

Anoop leaned back in his chair. "So where do we go from here?"

Bruce sighed heavily and articulated the dreaded, but logical next step. "We have to push Laney DeGraff a little harder on what she might know about the murders."

CHAPTER TWENTY-FIVE

Sandrine wrung her hands as she entered the remote monitor room next door to the room in which Laney was being interrogated. Detective MacRae had been with Laney for an hour and, thankfully, no one else was there. Her heart felt heavy that she was eavesdropping. Spying on Laney seemed tantamount to secretly rifling around in her purse, and self-reproach settled bitterly in her mouth.

As much as she wanted to know more, she was afraid to hear more. Nevertheless, her need to know everything, as painful as it was, was stronger than her dread of the unknown. She was emotionally invested in Laney, and listening in might help her decide whether she should completely pull out of this situation.

The professional in her screamed at her to run. No cop should associate with anyone who got clogged in the criminal quagmire. However, her heart screamed louder. She had never felt so close to the possibility of a relationship, which was precarious because it involved a woman who could go to prison. So why was her heart battling to believe Laney really wasn't as guilty as some of the evidence suggested?

The book, she remembered. Because none of this was written in the mental edition of the good-cop handbook that Bruce had told her about. If this situation wasn't in there, neither was the solution. But if it was, it would tell her to do all the things she didn't want to do. That's why Bruce said she should tear out the page and burn it.

Too nervous to sit, she stood close to the monitor that displayed Laney and Detective MacRae in stark black and white.

"…about two weeks before the art gallery opening," Laney was telling the detective.

"So how many times in those two weeks did you see Candace Dooring?"

"I saw her probably four times."

"Which times were those?"

"Twice at a place we," Laney hesitated, "they hang out. On Highland Avenue."

"That would be the Tire Store?"

"Yes."

"And where else?"

"Once at the Equinox and then the night at the art gallery."

Redirect, Sandrine silently willed Bruce.

"And you were with Candace that last night."

"We were leaving the opening at the same time. I walked her to her car."

"Where did she go after that?"

She touched her hand to her chest. "I have no idea. She drove off and then I walked to my car and went home."

"How long were you in the gallery with her?"

Laney paused, tilting her head upward as if trying to recall. "Not long. Half an hour, forty-five minutes, I suppose."

"And what do you remember about Candace?"

"She was nice. Easy to talk to. But I really didn't have any in-depth conversations with her."

Redirect. Come on, Bruce, redirect. Sandrine's heart felt like it would explode.

"Who knew her the best?"

"I would say that Theresa Aguilar did, though…"

"What is it?"

"The first night I met Candace, at the Equinox, she seemed aloof toward—"

"What about the Tire Store?" Detective MacRae suddenly said.

There's the redirection. Sandrine held her breath.

"Excuse me?"

"The Tire Store."

"Forgive me, Detective." Laney looked confused. "But before we move on, I was saying that at the Equinox that night, Candace acted aloof toward Theresa."

Sandrine blew out a sharply held breath of relief. Cops often used this ploy of changing the subject quickly if they were questioning someone they believed was lying. A liar would follow the new questioning eagerly and relax because the focus had shifted. An innocent person might become perplexed by the abrupt change in questioning and want to return to the previous subject.

"Aloof?"

Laney nodded. "She acted businesslike, as if something was going on between them."

"A personal thing, like an affair?"

"No, I don't think so."

"Did she mention any names?"

"No. But I think Candace was trying to warn me about the group. She told me to be careful."

"What else did she say?"

"That was it."

"Okay. Now, I want you to go over again what happened the night of her murder. Include every detail, even though we've been through this before."

Sandrine was convinced by what she was seeing in the monitor. Though Laney hadn't revealed much verbal proof, her expressions and body language screamed volumes. Aside from her reaction to the redirection of questioning, other compelling indicators were there. Her brows were furrowed in a sincere way that was entirely unconscious. She was looking directly into Bruce's eyes, which contradicted the behavior of a liar, who almost always avoided making eye contact. And liars typically didn't touch their chest or heart with an open hand, which Laney had also done.

"She's telling the truth," Sandrine said aloud. "About everything."

Being able to scrutinize Laney from her detached position had enabled her to remove a lot of her own feelings from the situation. She wasn't the one talking to her, so as a voyeur, she could be more objective. And what she saw answered so many troublesome, burning questions.

As Laney began to recount the night at the art gallery, Sandrine left the room. It was too hard to watch any more of the interrogation of the woman she had been intimate with. Detective MacRae would let her know if something new came up, and while it was prudent to pray that nothing did, Sandrine knew she wouldn't need to.

❖

It was almost midnight and the bank was dark except for the teller lights, left on for security reasons, and a single lamp in Laney's office. She sat behind her desk wondering how much longer she'd be able to call this place her own.

Years of memories flooded her mind, days when she was young and excited to be working for her father, and recent times when the responsibilities of an entire company rested directly on her shoulders. She had continued to build upon the success of the bank after she replaced her father. Revenues had risen at a constant pace and her customers were happy. She had personally helped so many wonderful people get into homes, purchase their first cars, and start their dream businesses.

She was proud of her accomplishments, and now one stupid night when she'd allowed poor judgment to influence her usual prudence had jeopardized it all. Letting the Pleasure Set into the bank was bad enough, but her carelessness with the security system had allowed Theresa to betray her trust and falsely implicate her in their crime.

She would visit her father in the morning and tell him everything. She had no idea how he would react, but she no longer cared about her fear. She was exhausted from worry and depressed about the debacle she'd created with Sandrine.

Goddamn it! She grew angrier realizing that one night of indiscretion would bring her down completely. At the very least, she might have to give up her position at the bank. At worst, she would go to prison. She stood up, too incensed to stay in her chair. Pacing around her office, she began to think out loud.

"That fucking bitch, using me and my bank. And implicating me!" Infuriated, she bent over the desk and pounded it with both fists. "You think you can destroy everything my father and I worked for all our lives?"

She stopped and stood upright. She was clenching her jaw so tight that a sharp pain shot up the sides of her face.

"Not on your fucking life."

❖

Sandrine had lain in bed awake for hours thinking about what had transpired over the past few days and the consequences that were now imminent. She had never strayed from standard police ethics and was as true blue as the movie versions of great Hollywood cops. Never had she questioned her actions, because the situations were always black and white. Good guys were good and bad guys were bad. Stealing was stealing.

But she was falling in love with Laney, and suddenly nothing was black and white. Laney was in trouble and the desire to help her went beyond her logical desire to serve and protect. Laney was unquestionably the one for her.

For the first time, she had decided to risk stepping outside of the line she had so resolutely drawn.

Like she was playing a game of chess, she mentally went over move after possible move. She then reset the board and tried another tactic. No matter which way she analyzed it, she kept returning to one single strategy. It was perilous, but she could envision only one clear way to a checkmate.

Her phone chirped from its holster by her bed. She glanced at the clock. It was 6:30 in the morning.

"I'm coming over," Laney was saying, and before Sandrine could respond, Laney said good-bye and hung up.

Laney was talking before Sandrine opened the door all the way. "Please, just hear me out for a minute. I know what you must be thinking, but my career might be ending and I'm fucking pissed. I know I've already lost you and, frankly, there's not a whole lot else to lose at this point. And all of this because I was a thickheaded, trusting idiot. I didn't see what they were planning and I stupidly opened my bank to them so they could fuck me for their own gain."

"Laney," Sandrine tried to interject.

"I've been in the banking business all my life and didn't even see this coming. I went to my father early this morning and told him everything. He's shocked and disappointed, but he stands behind me. And to think that I had to go to him in shame all because Theresa Aguilar cast her manipulative eye on me and conned me right up the ass."

"Laney."

"I'm not going to let her get away with this."

"Laney."

"I'm going to get the tape."

"What?"

"I'm going to get the tape."

"Wait." Sandrine pulled Laney through the door and to her living room. "Sit down."

Laney was visibly tense and it looked like she'd been up all night. They both took a seat. Laney balled up her hands and Sandrine watched the blood drain from her knuckles. "Just calm down a bit. Would you like some water? Coffee?'

"No, not just yet, thank you," Laney said as she stared at the carpet.

"Okay. So, how do you plan to get the tape?"

"I'm not sure, but I'll do whatever it takes."

Sandrine placed her hand over one of Laney's fists. Slowly, Laney relaxed and allowed Sandrine to clasp her hands.

Laney began to breathe more slowly, but she was still looking down at the carpet when she said quietly, "I'm so sorry for all that has happened between you and me. I've betrayed your trust and ruined the friendship we've had for years."

Sandrine had spent the night thinking about what she had observed at Laney's interrogation. She had certainly gotten into a mess, but it had not been premeditated. Red flags were flying around everywhere, some because of Laney's revelations, but some were as old as Sandrine's emotional scars. She had every reason to walk away from this relationship, but she couldn't. Sandrine hooked a finger under Laney's chin and lifted her face so she could look into her eyes.

Sandrine could remain protected and stay away from Laney and her problems, or she could go with her heart and trust that what they had together was more important than the problems. She recalled her father's recent words. His deep, comforting voice came through clearly. *Love is not perfect*, he had said.

"Laney, I have done a lot of thinking about this. Admittedly, I was shocked when I found out all that was going on with you and Theresa. You and I had just begun to get to know each other better. I've always liked you, and over the years I came to really like you. And when I started having a chance to pursue my deeper feelings for you, I was crushed when everything exploded."

Laney began to interrupt but Sandrine said, "Please let me finish. I'm not asking you for an apology or an excuse. I think I understand the things you've done but, more importantly, the things you haven't done. I believe you when you say you didn't know about Theresa's plans."

"You do?"

Laney had such a pained look on her face, Sandrine wanted to hold her and show her how deeply she felt, but she needed to finish before her childhood fears took over.

"I do. And I want you to know that I don't want to lose you. I want to see where this goes with you and me. Because of that, I'm planning to request that someone take over the laundering case. It wouldn't be ethical for me to work it and be with you."

"I don't want you to compromise your assignments."

"That's okay. There are other fraud detectives in the department. And besides, it'll be turned over to the Treasury Department soon enough, thanks to the evidence you've provided. I'll make sure everyone knows you were the one that brought it to the police."

"Thank you," Laney said softly.

"I'm here for you. And we'll get through this."

A pale blush washed over Laney's face. She looked like she was about to crumple from stress.

"You know where my bed is. Please go lie down for a little while. I'll make some coffee."

Laney hesitated and Sandrine presumed she was about to say something like she'd already bothered her too much or had taken up too much of her time. But she just stood there, looking so tired. Her eyes were glossed over and her skin had turned ashen.

Sandrine coaxed her with a smile. "Go."

❖

Sandrine returned with the coffee and saw that Laney was lying on the bed, face-down. She wasn't asleep but she seemed to have relaxed a little. Sandrine placed the mugs on the nightstand.

"You're beautiful," Sandrine said, and lowered herself onto the bed and on top of Laney. Reaching underneath Laney's armpits and up her forearms, she clasped her wrists and slowly brought her full body weight down onto her back. She buried her face in Laney's hair and closed her eyes to take in the feel of the entire length of her body. She was warm and soon Sandrine's breathing matched the rise and fall of Laney's.

"I feel safe here," Laney said.

Sandrine ached for her. "I'll keep you safe."

Laney kissed Sandrine's forearm, nuzzling her lips across her skin. Sandrine opened her eyes and tightened her embrace. Simultaneously, they let out sighs of contentment. In that moment, they were together and alone, with none of the worries that had threatened them invading their world.

Gradually, Laney's hips began to move underneath Sandrine

and Sandrine's body stirred in response. She studied the hand nestled in her grip. This was the same slender, sexy hand she had seen many times in Laney's office. It was the same hand that signed paperwork, gestured to make a point, or opened her office door. And now, this hand, and the rest of her, wasn't responding to the activities of daily business but to Sandrine.

Laney turned over to face Sandrine and their bodies fit with a complete rightness. As Laney's hips resumed their slow gyration, Sandrine pressed back and their dance began. It was a slow dance of discovery as they began to move from friendly familiarity to a slowly evolving intimacy. Their kisses were slow and deliberate while they moved together with an instinctive rhythm that complemented the slow swirling of their tongues.

It was as if Sandrine already knew Laney's every curve and hard and soft spots. The excitement of exploring her so intimately was amazing but also strangely familiar. It wasn't just from the last time Laney was here, when Laney had first touched her. It was deeper and much more profound. It wasn't from intently observing Laney in the years she had known her. In the most pure and essential way, Sandrine's body simply recognized Laney's. It wasn't enough to merely say they fit together. The way Laney moved with her and the ease with which their arms and legs found just the right places together differentiated Laney from all the other women Sandrine had ever been with.

The sensation of familiarity somehow preceded their first meeting and surged through her at a cellular level.

Sandrine buried her head in Laney's neck, the soft blond hair sweeping over her cheeks like a silky kerchief. She opened her mouth to Laney's neck and her throat tightened. Tears rose from a profound place. Laney moaned and pushed her hips more emphatically into Sandrine. A swirling sensation expanded between her legs and her excitement rose.

No longer did her clothes, or Laney's, feel right. Sandrine had to lie skin to skin with her, to feel true intimacy. She sat up and pulled her nightshirt over her head.

"Is this okay?" Sandrine said, a little too late.

"Yes." Laney wiped a tear from Sandrine's face. "We can stop," she almost whispered.

Sandrine shook her head.

Slowly, Laney moved her hands down and caressed Sandrine's breasts as gently as a child explores a butterfly. Light fingers danced across her skin, raising goose bumps over Sandrine's entire upper body. As Laney withdrew her hands, Sandrine shivered and wrapped her arms tightly across her chest. Her breathing grew more rapid and she wondered if she would explode from the inside. She felt raw and bare. She knew now that her fears, her anguish, and her desires were out in the open.

Laney seemed to understand every emotion cascading through Sandrine. She removed her own shirt and remained still while Sandrine calmed her breathing and the trembling subsided. Without speaking, she had exposed herself as well, understanding Sandrine's need to be vulnerable together.

Sandrine lowered her head onto Laney's shoulder. The feel of Laney's hands as they tenderly stroked her hair was the beginning of her own absolution from the darkness her heart had been locked inside.

Her tears fell, landing silently on Laney's shoulder.

After a long while, Sandrine lifted herself up and smiled as she took a deep breath. She raised her hand, taking Laney's into hers, and guided it toward her breast. When she dropped her own hand, she was allowing Laney to be their only physical connection. *Trust.* Sandrine called for strength from within. *Trust this woman in front of you. Let it happen.*

And as Laney softly caressed her, the tears that rolled down Sandrine's face spoke of a new kind of release. She had taken the keys she had held all along and unlocked the door to her prison of distrust. And in that moment, she allowed herself to become lost in the exact place where their hearts had found each other.

CHAPTER TWENTY-SIX

Laney awoke alone in Sandrine's bed and checked her watch. It was almost eleven o'clock in the morning. She had fallen asleep for an hour and a half. Though she was still dead tired, the nap made her feel better.

Walking through the house to look for Sandrine, she took in the warm-colored walls and deep brown hardwood floors that made this Sandrine's place. Beautiful paintings adorned all the rooms and a fresh bouquet of flowers sat on the dining-room table. She wandered into the kitchen, which was designed in a French provincial country theme with rustic white wood cabinets and earthy granite countertops that housed terra-cotta pottery.

Wondering where Sandrine was, she finally spotted her outside sitting at a teak patio set.

"Hey." Laney stepped outside and sat next to her.

Sandrine took Laney's hand. "Hi. I didn't want to wake you so I came out here."

"I really crashed. I'm sorry."

"You were tired." Sandrine's eyes squinted as an affectionate smile emerged. But soon Sandrine's expression began to cloud over.

"Are you okay?"

"I am." Sandrine touched her arm. "We are." As she drew her hand away, she said, "I called my lieutenant a little while ago and told him to reassign the fraud case. He asked why and I told him that I knew you and didn't want to compromise the investigation."

"So, is that a good thing?"

"It is now." She kissed Laney. "Especially after this morning."

Laney smiled. "But you look troubled."

"I *am* troubled about what I am going to say next."

Laney braced for bad news. "What is it, Sandrine?"

"I'm going to help you get out of this mess."

"What do you mean?"

"I want to help you collect evidence that exonerates you. Then you can turn it over to the police so Theresa can't use the tape against you."

"The tape," Laney said. She hadn't thought about the damning piece of video all morning.

"Since the tape needs encryption software to copy it, I'm fairly sure there's only the one master. Nevertheless, she still has power while she holds it. The only way to refute the tape is to get something on her that renders it useless."

"Are you sure you want to do that, Sandrine?"

"I sat here a long time asking myself the same question. Part of me is screaming to not get involved, but I *am* involved. With you. And you're involved with this. I believe you've been blackmailed. This was a premeditated move on Theresa's part and she absolutely won't hesitate to use it to get what she wants. And if she feels that she's going down, she'll try to bring you down with her."

"I don't want you to get into trouble."

"And I don't want you to get into trouble, either."

They regarded each other silently. The sun penetrated through the palm trees in Sandrine's backyard and the rays fell across the teak table and Sandrine's arms. She was beautiful and she was doing this for her. The gratitude and affection that suddenly began to flow in every part of Laney's being was growing into love.

Laney took her hand. "It all sounds risky."

"It is. But without solid evidence that contradicts the tape, I'm not sure you'd ever be able to prove your innocence."

"And what kind of evidence would that be?"

Sandrine stood and wrapped her arms around Laney. She nuzzled her neck and kissed her ear. "Let's take a shower and then I'll show you."

❖

"We're going to visit a friend," Sandrine said when they were out the door and in Sandrine's car.

Laney wasn't sure what that meant, but she fully trusted her. "Sounds clandestine."

"It is, in a way. Her name is Gadget Girl. I've used her in the past when the department's equipment wasn't what I needed for investigations."

"A real-life Q."

"Pardon?"

"The guy who supplies James Bond with all his gadgets."

"Well, Gadget Girl probably doesn't have shoes equipped with daggers, but she does have a lot of toys that are just as useful."

They pulled up to an apartment in West Hollywood, an older Spanish-style building covered with ivy. They walked to number thirteen and rang the buzzer.

Promptly, the door opened and standing there was a short, plump woman about thirty years old. Clothed in designer jeans, she wore a black T-shirt that read THERE'S TOO MUCH BLOOD IN MY ALCOHOL SYSTEM.

"Laney, this is Gadget Girl. Gadget Girl, this is Laney."

"Nice to meetcha. Come on in, Detective."

Laney had imagined a dark place with windows drawn tight and a messy interior full of stacks of old magazines and take-out food containers, but the apartment was sunny and immaculate. Expensive furniture and a couple of bookcases, full of exceedingly well-organized contents, shared the main room with an elegant glass table upon which sat an impressive computer system.

Gadget Girl motioned them to the forest green leather couch while she took a seat in a mission-style armchair.

"What can I do for you?" she said.

"We need to capture some conversations," Sandrine replied.

"Stealth recorder or listening device?"

Sandrine thought a moment. "Our target might be too sly and check for a body bug, but we have a challenge with the location."

"Which is?"

"A house."

"Bag job?"

"No, there won't be any break-ins."

"Command of target?"

Laney was scarcely able to follow the secret spy conversation.

"Probably not. I'll be close by but not within visual range."

Gadget Girl looked at Laney. "Is she the acorn?"

"Yes."

"Hmmm," Gadget Girl said. "A parabolic microphone, then?"

"Through a window, possibly."

"An open window is best.What will the take be?"

"A recorded conversation. No video needed."

Gadget Girl got up and went into another room. She returned shortly with a box the size of a large toaster oven.

"This is a long-range parabolic microphone. Newest toy I have. Not even on the consumer market yet. It's equipped with a three-band equalizer to adjust for specific sound frequencies. All you do is snap together the six-panel dish."

She handed the box to Sandrine.

"It's got a twelve-hundred-foot line-of-sight pickup range, so just focus it straight in the direction of the sound. It won't go through walls that well, though. Oh, and there's an output jack for taping the conversation. Think that'll do ya?"

Sandrine looked down at the box, nodding silently.

Gadget Girl tilted her chin toward Laney. "Wanna try a button mic instead?"

"No. The transmitter would be too bulky for this job. It's more a close-range target." Sandrine looked at Laney with apprehension.

While the conversation sounded Greek to Laney, she did understand that the reference to "close-range" meant Theresa's proximity to her.

Back at Sandrine's place, Laney sat with her while she put together the parabolic microphone. It looked more like a contraption for a low-budget horror movie, but Laney was enthralled when it was assembled.

"This baby should do the trick," Sandrine said.

"How does it work?"

"This is a super-sensitive microphone that can pick up sounds. As long as I'm close by, I'll be able to record your conversation with Theresa. The key will be to try to find direct access. Hopefully an open window."

Laney wondered how that would come about.

"Now, I need you to start going into different rooms and talking quietly so I can test this."

The plan was in place. Laney walked out of her bedroom dressed in a black pantsuit with a green top. It was understated but she felt comfortable wearing it, and she truly needed all the comfort she could muster. Her hands shook and she was tempted to throw back a couple shots of whiskey, but she needed her thinking to be clear.

Her cell phone rang and the sound rattled her.

"Laney, it's Sandrine."

"Hi."

"You're nervous."

"A little. Well, a lot."

"We should call this off."

"No, I want to do it."

"Are you sure?"

"Yes."

"Still, I'm not sure I should be putting you in possible jeopardy."

"Sandrine, I need to do this."

After a long silence, Sandrine said, "Do you have the windows open?"

"Both the living room and bedroom windows, yes."

"Good. I'm on my way and will be parked down the street until Theresa arrives. Just stay as calm as possible or Theresa will know something's up."

"Okay." All Laney had to do was engage Theresa in conversation about the tape and get her to admit that she'd framed her. If Sandrine was successful, she'd have it all on tape. *All she had to do.* It sounded simple but her apprehension was justified. Theresa was a cunning, deceitful con artist and, Laney reasoned, a seasoned villain that she wasn't well equipped to lock horns with.

"Just follow our plan. I've done this a lot of times. If at any time you feel like things are getting out of control, just say 'stop right now.' I'll hear you and come get you. It's not worth risking your well-being for this, do you understand?"

"Yes."

"I'll be there soon. And Laney?" Sandrine's voice wavered a little. "Please be careful."

"I will."

Laney hung up, walked into her living room, and sat on the couch. Shakily, she checked her watch. Theresa was due to arrive in less than twenty minutes. She held her hands out and examined the tremors.

Laney was numb. She had gotten into so much trouble, all because she thought her glamorous new friends were strong, capable women. She had been pulled, like a stupid, powerless pile of iron shavings, toward the magnetic strength of the Pleasure Set. It had seduced her to make foolish decisions and neglect her friends. The loss of sleep made her work suffer and, now, she was facing the obliteration of her lifelong career.

Her throat closed and hot tears of shame began to well up in her eyes. She pictured the horrible embarrassment and shame she would face if she had to resign, empty her office, and bear all the shocked and disappointed looks of her employees. Exasperated, she swiped at her tears.

She looked around the house at all the things she'd worked

so hard for. She thought about Sandrine, out on the street, risking departmental punishment for her.

Suddenly anger burst inside her. *Stop this! Theresa fucked you over. You trusted her friendship and look what she did to you. Goddamn her! Do what you have to catch her and send her away.*

An acerbic taste rose in her throat. As her anger escalated, her hands stopped shaking and a more constructive type of energy took over and empowered her. *This is good. Use this to mask your nervousness.*

CHAPTER TWENTY-SEVEN

Sandrine, parked on Laney's street, sat with her hand on the parabolic microphone. Her nerves were on edge, the tingling of anticipation more about Laney's well-being than about catching Theresa.

Maybe she shouldn't have allowed Laney to participate in this sting, but it seemed the only way to vindicate her. They would simply have a conversation, she kept telling herself. It shouldn't get out of hand. She would record the incriminating evidence and then hand it over to Laney to take to the new agent assigned to the fraud case.

But in the back of her mind, she knew Theresa was very likely involved in the two murders and feared that she wouldn't hesitate to hurt Laney. As soon as they collected the evidence, Laney would have to lay low and avoid being Theresa's next target.

She also debated her own involvement in this scheme. It was highly unscrupulous and risky for her as well. She didn't have a court order to gather this kind of evidence against Theresa, but as long as Laney didn't reveal the source of her recordings, Sandrine wouldn't appear to be involved.

For the first time in her life, she had put her career in jeopardy. But she couldn't stand by and watch Laney go down with the felons of the Pleasure Set.

A black BMW glided up the street and parked on the curb by Laney's house. Sandrine's heart jumped into double time as she watched Theresa get out and head toward the house. When Laney opened the door and let her in, Sandrine grabbed the equipment and headed for the back of the house.

"Why the change of heart?" Theresa didn't waste time confronting Laney about her sudden invitation.

Laney directed her to the couch in the living room, close to the open window. Sandrine shouldn't have a problem sneaking up to it because the redwood deck right outside would soften her footsteps. "It's not so much a change of heart, but an opportunity I thought up."

"Meaning?"

"First of all, if you repeat any of this, I'll deny it. I haven't yet told the police anything they can use," she said, the lie rolling easily off her tongue, "but I want to make sure we understand each other first." Taking an offensive stance right off had been Sandrine's idea, and it bolstered her confidence.

Theresa nodded, though her expression remained unreadable. "I'm listening."

"I believe I can explain to the police about your bank accounts."

"And how would you do that?"

"Account for the deposits and point them toward Morgan's gallery to show them the receipts of the legitimate purchases." Laney fought to not sarcastically spit out the word *legitimate* since it was complete bullshit.

"Would that call the police off?"

"It should. They'd listen to a bank president, especially if she knew the customer personally and if you have a clean record. Do you?"

Theresa's laugh sounded chillingly sardonic. "Of course."

"Then the police will probably drop the case."

"Okay. So I know what you would do. More importantly, why would you do it?"

Laney wanted to glare at Theresa. She wanted to rip her eyes out. Instead, she simply answered, "I want the tape back."

Theresa stood and pulled Laney by the hand, making her stand as well. "First of all, I've needed to apologize for everything." To Laney's surprise, she hugged her. Laney let it happen and the embrace was tight. Theresa's full body was pressed up against her and Theresa rubbed her back. With sudden terror, Laney realized Theresa was in fact looking for a bug. That was exactly why Sandrine had declined the offer from Gadget Girl. The hug unnerved her and she fought her rising anxiety.

You don't have a bug on you, she reassured herself, *so calm down.*

Full of contempt, she rubbed Theresa's back, all the while cursing her for her deviousness. Theresa moved one hand to Laney's chest and rubbed the spot between her breasts. She must have been satisfied that Laney wasn't wearing a recording device because she pulled back smiling.

Fuck, Laney thought. *That was a close call. I'm out of the woods for now.*

Theresa took her hand and started for the kitchen.

"Where are we going?" Forewarning prickles scurried up the back of Laney's neck.

Theresa didn't respond but walked her through the kitchen and opened her garage door. They stepped in and Laney's fear grew rapidly because they were quickly moving out of Sandrine's range.

❖

What the fuck is she doing? Sandrine thought as the voices moved away from the living room. She had set up the parabolic microphone easily and, from her crouched position below the window, had recorded Laney and Theresa's discussion. Her earphone had assured her that the conversation was clear and understandable. She had simply been sitting still, hoping Theresa gave them what they needed. But suddenly things had changed.

She must be moving her away in case she thinks there's a bug in the room. Sandrine risked lifting her head and, as she peeked through the window, she saw Laney stepping through a door off the kitchen.

She quickly backed up until she was away from the window and moved around the house in the direction the women had gone. The contraption was a bit cumbersome, but she had to reposition herself if possible. Finding the kitchen window, she continued around the house and realized Theresa had taken Laney into the garage.

Damn! No windows. She scrambled to the front of the garage, looking around quickly to make sure no neighbors would see her and ask what she was doing. Any shout from a neighbor would tip Theresa off that something was going on. She checked the seal at the bottom of the garage door but couldn't find an open gap to place the microphone up against.

Beads of sweat dripped from her temples. She had to think fast. She returned to the side of the house and considered crawling through the living-room window to get closer to the inside door to the garage, but that would put the plan in high risk of failure. Where would she be able to hide but still get close enough to the door to pick up the voices? If Theresa exited quickly she would catch Sandrine.

But what was her other choice?

Her sense of urgency was high, and she had to swallow the panic that rose in her throat. She had to go in.

As she made her way back around the side of the garage, a flash of white caught her eye. Next to a low-lying bush against the side of the house was a vent—the dryer vent. She had been so determined to get to the front of the garage, she had missed it entirely.

Would it work? She dropped to her knees and shoved the microphone as far up into the vent as possible. She could hear their voices.

What dialogue had she missed? It was too late to worry. At least they were back in business as long as one particular thing didn't happen. *Please don't turn on the dryer.*

❖

"This is silly." Laney was trying to prolong the conversation, hoping Sandrine figured out what had just happened. "Why would you take me out here?"

"In case someone came to the door. I don't want to be interrupted."

Theresa's excuse was bullshit, Laney thought. She probably believed there was a bug somewhere in the house and had found a place where no one would think to place one. Theresa was extremely smart, and Laney teetered on the verge of giving in to the fear that she was in way over her head. *Keep angry, just keep angry.*

"Look, I've already put myself in a really bad position, so don't play around with me anymore."

"I'm not trying to, darling."

"So why all this clandestine shit?" Laney waved her arm around the garage, knowing she'd stalled just about long enough.

"Maybe I've seen too many movies."

"What does that mean?"

"Clandestine maneuvers, making deals that could benefit us both." Theresa smiled. "It's a Hollywood tradition."

"Speaking of making deals, like I said, I want the tape back."

"So let's talk. You know I'd like to give it back, but for now I can't."

"Why would you keep the tape to use against me when you know I had no knowledge of your plans?"

"It was just a bit of insurance."

"Insurance for what?"

"That we could not only have some fun together, but do a little business as well."

"But you turned the camera on deliberately. I had no idea."

Theresa chuckled. "No, you didn't. You're too innocent, Laney. I can't believe you were born and raised in Beverly Hills, the daughter of a bank president, no less, and remained so naïve."

"Well, I'm not so naïve now. Let's just face the facts that you wanted to launder money in my bank without my knowledge."

"Yes." She sounded bored. "And?"

"You stole that tape to make it look like I was involved."

Theresa didn't respond.

"Why would you do that? Weren't we friends?"

"Of course we are, Laney. But you never would have gone along until you realized that we weren't really harming anyone in the process."

"You're endangering my reputation. I could lose my bank."

"You won't. Just cooperate and everything will be fine."

"It feels like blackmail, Theresa. After the time we've spent together, this really hurts." *Would she buy that?*

"I knew you wouldn't let us keep those accounts open, so until I could convince you that everything was okay, I needed to make sure I could hold your attention."

"Well, you've got it now."

"Please don't be angry, Laney. It's not as bad as you think. As long as your offer still stands to tell the police you've checked us out and your employee jumped the gun in reporting the accounts, we should all be fine."

Laney pretended to ponder this. "So you're offering that we become business partners, so to speak."

"Yes, I am."

"If I agree to this, you have to let me in on everything."

"Of course."

"Okay." Laney took a deep breath, since she was about to go off script. "Tell me what happened to Candace."

❖

No! Sandrine almost yelled out loud. They already had enough evidence to exonerate Laney. So what the fuck was she doing now? She wasn't supposed to go any further. And now she was pushing Theresa for more. The hair stood up on the nape of her neck, and she recognized forewarning.

She steadied the microphone so it wouldn't fall out of the dryer vent, pulled her cell phone from its cradle, and moved away from the garage wall. She'd be away from the earphones for a less than a minute but prayed nothing would happen in that scant but dangerous time.

❖

"Candace?" Theresa's brow furrowed.

"She was unhappy about the group. She told me so the night she died."

"The police are trying to find out, Laney."

"Why did she want out of the group? And why was she going to the police?"

"She told you that?"

"Yes, she did." She hadn't, but Laney needed to push her.

"Look, I'm as upset as you are about her death—"

"Theresa, cut the bullshit. She knew something and was about to go to the police. If I'm going to partner with you on this, I need to know what I'm getting into."

Theresa's eyes glazed over and the side of her mouth twitched. "You're not getting into anything more than we talked about."

"Is it about the heroin?"

Theresa almost evaded a facial reaction, but Laney saw that the shock had registered.

"The heroin?"

"Kay told me about it all. That's how you're making so much money." Now she had to convince Theresa it was just business talk. "I don't care what you do to make money. But you need to keep the heroin sales as far away from my bank as you can. Are you going directly from the drug sales to the art gallery? There'd better be other steps in between to clean the money."

Theresa stared at her for what seemed like five minutes. Light-headed, Laney knew she had stepped in way too deep. But she couldn't go back now. Her ears pounded and she was afraid she might faint. She was too nervous to wait out the silence. "I hope you're being smart about the money trail. You can't just go from street sales through the gallery and into the bank. Tell me you're not being that stupid, because I won't be a part of such an obtuse, rudimentary plan."

Theresa's eyes tensed into slits as if she was debating her next words. "It seems you've done your homework."

"Homework? Banking is my life. I've seen this before and I probably know more about money laundering than you'll ever understand. Please don't insult me."

Going on the offensive seemed to work.

"I'm not, Laney. Everything is set up very well. All you need to worry about is the end result."

"If I can easily trace the money trail, so can a lot of other people."

"But no one has."

"Candace did. That's why she was about to go to the police."

"Candace didn't know about the laundering."

"Then why was she going to go to the police?"

"She knew about the heroin."

"And that got her killed?"

"I can't control the front end."

"So, you're saying that Jimmy Pick killed her?"

Theresa laughed. "I don't know who killed her, Laney. But since you seem to know all the players involved, why don't you ask them?"

"Because I'm asking you." Laney's anger started to come from a genuine place now. The woman standing in front of her obviously didn't care who died. Laney's voice rose. "Because Candace is dead and it's all a little too fucking close to my bank."

"Take it easy, Laney."

"Take it easy? Candace was murdered because she knew about the front end of this plan. And you invited me to a party that took place in the house of another dead woman. And a member of our group. Did Bridget know about the heroin as well?"

Theresa held up a hand. "Look, things happen, Laney. But all of this won't affect you. As far as anyone's concerned, all you do is run a bank."

"But heroin, Theresa. Jesus. Do you really need the money from the heroin sales to help enlarge the bankroll you're keeping from your husband?"

Theresa's laughter sounded maniacal as it echoed against the hard surfaces in the garage. "Need the money? We don't need the money. We do it because we can. We can get away with things no one else can. Remember? We're fucking the system. No one suspects us and we can do any fucking thing we want. Plus, what else do you do in your life that's this exciting?"

Laney reeled from Theresa's sudden admission that the story about keeping bank accounts secret from their husbands and boyfriends was bogus. This group of elitist women believed they were so superior that they could get away with anything just to satisfy the monotony of their rich lives and entertain themselves at the cost of others. Laney felt the sour tang of disgust rise in her throat.

Theresa leaned close to her. "You keep the police away from our accounts and everything will be okay."

"Why am I not convinced? Either you aren't in control of the front-end heroin operation or you are but you don't want to truly partner with me and would rather keep me in the dark. Either scenario is too much of a risk for me."

"You'll get the tape back. Then there'll be no risk to you as long as you act ignorant."

Once more, she avoided giving Laney a direct answer.

"I'm not dim-witted enough to believe that you'll give me the tape back until you're done using my bank and have moved on."

Theresa crossed her arms. "Okay. What do you want?"

So far, her coolness had gotten her a lot of information. She prayed that Sandrine was somewhere getting all of this. But if not, Laney would nonetheless be able to serve as a witness. She crossed her arms, mimicking Theresa, and went for it all.

"I want to know everyone involved in this little plan of yours."

"You don't need to know it all."

"Then maybe you don't need my bank."

"Laney, don't ruin this. You'll still be able to party with us and have the kind of fun you've been enjoying. How many people get to go the places we go and do the things we do? You're in with the most privileged and influential group around. Take advantage of that and let me take care of the rest."

"I don't know," Laney said. "This is all too dicey. You're going to have to do better than that or I'll have to reconsider."

A startling flash in Theresa's expression revealed either fury or hostility. Before Laney could react, Theresa grabbed Laney's shirt in her fist and shoved her up against the garage wall. A metal shovel that had been hanging nearby fell, hitting the floor with a loud clatter. Laney's back hit something hard and she winced.

"I've had enough of your little power play, Laney." Theresa had turned vile so unexpectedly that Laney sucked in a stunned breath. She was yelling now, and the fist that forcefully grasped her shirt pushed painfully into her chest. "You think you have some bargaining power here? All of the control is in my court, you stupid little bitch. As long as I hold the tape, you're in this scheme right along with me."

Theresa was so close to her now that she could smell sweat mixing with perfume. The spicy fragrance that had seemed so refreshing when they'd first met now smelled putrid. Laney felt beads of sweat form on her forehead. Theresa was fuming and Laney knew she had pushed her too far. But she was also livid and no longer cared that Theresa was threatening her. The only thing to do now was push her even further.

"I'm out of the group, Theresa. You're on your own. I don't give a shit about the tape anymore. Use it, for all I care, because you can't do anything to me. And your power plays are getting really fucking boring. Did Bridget get bored with you, too? Did her bank also realize that your operation was mediocre, at best? You think you're such a big player, but your grand scheme is laughable. Go find another bank to fuck with."

Something jabbed Laney's ribs. Theresa had thrust a handgun against her. With every few syllables Theresa spoke, she jammed the gun into Laney's ribs for emphasis. "I'm not fucking around with your little games anymore. Don't try to challenge me or you'll end up eating my gun like Bridget and Candace did. There, you wanted to be a partner? Now you're part of this. Both of those idiots tried to go to the police, so they were the laughable ones."

She stepped back, pushing hard off Laney's breasts as she did so.

❖

Sandrine jumped as soon as she heard a crash. She reached up to remove her earphone so she could detach from the parabolic contraption and get to Laney, but something told her to stay put and listen. Laney hadn't said "stop right now," the code phrase for Sandrine to come and help, so she hung back. She could be there in seconds if she needed to. And as she listened to the ensuing conversation, Laney's surprising mettle amazed her. She had pushed Theresa too far and the next few sentences sealed Theresa's fate. But now, Theresa was threatening her.

Was Theresa going to beat her up? Did she have a gun?

That was enough, Sandrine decided. She put the equipment down, with its microphone still shoved into the vent, and raced around to the front of the house.

❖

Theresa and Laney faced off in silence, and Laney tried to fight back the terror she felt creeping onto her face. She hadn't refused to use the code phrase. In her anger, she had actually forgotten to.

Neither said anything as they both remained frozen with only their breathing showing any movement between them.

The doorbell rang and Theresa turned her head toward the sound. "They'll go away."

It rang again. A muffled voice said, "Laney?"

Laney almost called out loud to Sandrine. She wanted to run to her or yell for help, but she was locked in a treacherous standoff. All Theresa would have to do was squeeze her finger less than an inch to pull the trigger. But knowing someone was at the door, Laney gambled that she wouldn't. She pushed past Theresa. "It's time for you to go." Sweat was now rolling down her face as she found the courage to walk out of the garage. With every step that carried her closer to Sandrine, she cringed in anticipation of a gunshot that would rip through her brain. Instead, Theresa followed her to the front door.

Laney swung the door open, and Sandrine stood there, smiling. "Come on, we're late for the lunch. And you know how Karen hates it when we're late." She looked past Laney and said, "Oh! Hi, Mrs. Aguilar. Sorry to disturb."

Theresa had lost her sinister expression. "Actually, I was just leaving." She hugged Laney and said close to her ear, "If this bitch police woman is your new girlfriend, you're more stupid than I thought. And I suggest you don't make any more stupid fucking moves."

When Theresa moved away from Laney, Sandrine stepped in, blocking her path. "I think you should go with us." Sandrine's eyes never left Theresa's as she added, "Laney, go get your purse. Now."

Confused, but comprehending the seriousness in Sandrine's expression, Laney backed away from the door about fifteen paces. She was now in the living room but could see the concentration on Sandrine's face.

"Thank you, really, Detective," Theresa said. "But I have to go."

"Are you sure?"

"Positive." She looked Sandrine up and down as if she were contemplating a future conquest. "Perhaps we could get together some other time."

As Theresa began to step around her, Sandrine wrenched her arm backward, throwing her off balance. Theresa tried to jerk her arm away. "What the fuck are you doing?"

Sandrine grabbed a handful of her hair and yanked her roughly to the ground. Theresa landed on her side and Sandrine pushed her onto her face and dropped a knee forcefully into Theresa's back, saying, "Oh, I think we should get together a lot sooner than that."

The *whoop whoop* of a police siren screeched suddenly, and Laney looked up to see Detective MacRae jumping out of a squad car and running down the front walk.

"She's got a gun," Laney yelled as MacRae ran toward the door.

MacRae pounced on Theresa and held her arms while Sandrine finished handcuffing her. They searched Theresa rather roughly until Sandrine located and secured the handgun in her pocket.

As both detectives began to stand up, Sandrine pushed off Theresa's back. Theresa grunted loudly, yelling, "Goddamn bitch! What the fuck is this?"

Sandrine stood over the prone woman. "You are being arrested for money laundering, blackmail, assault with a handgun, and for the murders of Bridget Marina and Candace Dooring." She then knelt down next to Theresa's head. "And for messing with my girlfriend, you fucking slime ball."

MacRae made a radio call. "We need a squad car with a female officer to take a suspect in."

"I can finish this, Bruce," Sandrine said.

"You're off the case, remember?" He smiled and nodded toward Laney. "Just get her down to the station to make her statement."

Sandrine stood up and looked at Laney. She stepped over Theresa and reached for her, taking her hand.

"And Girard," MacRae said, "Remember what I said about the mental edition of the good-cop handbook?"

Sandrine nodded.

"Now's the time to tear out that page and burn it."

Laney didn't know what they meant but she knew it had something to do with her. She watched as MacRae reached down and lifted Theresa to her feet. Her face was red, her hair badly disheveled, and her eyes bulged, making her look deranged. She suddenly screamed at Laney. "You fuckin' set me up!"

Sandrine's hand felt warm and secure in hers. Whatever

happened now, at least Theresa's arrogant scheme had been blown to smithereens. Laney shrugged. "It's a Hollywood tradition."

❖

Once backup had taken Theresa away, Laney took Sandrine inside, and when she closed the door, Sandrine erupted.

"What do you think you were doing? She was threatening you. She could have hurt you."

Laney had been so angry she hadn't even considered that Theresa had used the gun before and could have easily used it just then. Her legs began to shake and she felt faint as she grasped the reality of what could have happened. "I need to sit down."

Sandrine scooped an arm under hers and led her to the couch. "Laney, you were just supposed to get her to admit that you weren't involved."

"But now she's admitted to killing Bridget and Candace. And she also knows about the heroin."

Sandrine threw her arms around her so tight that Laney couldn't breathe. "I could have lost you, damn it."

"But you didn't. Listen, I got into this jam and, more than wanting to get out of it, I want her to pay the price, for me and for Bridget and Candace."

Sandrine sat back and wiped her own forehead, which was dripping with sweat. Laney saw how scared Sandrine really was and a slow-rolling rush came over her. What had just happened could have gone horribly wrong.

"I'm sorry. It was stupid to goad Theresa. I've screwed up enough so far and I realize now that Theresa's gun could have permanently ruined everything."

Sandrine's eyes welled up and, in that moment, Laney understood how deeply they were now connected. She stroked back a lock of Sandrine's damp hair. "I love you."

Sandrine blinked and a tear spilled out and down her cheek. "I love you, too."

Laney pulled Sandrine into a hug and they stayed there for a long while as Laney squeezed her eyes shut, the extreme weight of her love for Sandrine starting to crash down on her.

After a while, Sandrine said quietly, "I was right outside the garage wall. I heard the crash but didn't know what had happened."

"And you came to my rescue."

"I had to. You were acting like the Lone Ranger in there."

"But you got everything on tape?"

"I did. However, I almost stopped this whole scheme earlier when you decided to carry the questioning a little too far."

"I needed to know more. I want her to get slammed for everything."

"It was foolish, Laney. She could have hurt you. I couldn't bear that. It was stupid of me to even think about recording your conversation." She held her tight and sighed. Laney cradled the back of Sandrine's head in her hands. It seemed they had overcome a hurdle. She wasn't sure where it would all lead, but Sandrine was still in her life, and that's all that mattered.

"But we did get the recording. And it's over."

Sandrine sat back and stroked Laney's cheek. "It's far from over."

"I'm scared."

"I know, baby. You have been through a lot. But as soon as I return the equipment to Gadget Girl and have her make copies of the recording, you can turn one over to the detective now on the case."

"And what about you? Are you going to get into trouble for helping me?"

"Possibly."

"Could you get fired?"

"I doubt it. I may get a reprimand or get time off without pay."

"That would be awful."

"Seeing you go to prison would have been awful." Sandrine tilted her head as she gave Laney a stern look. "I hope this is the end of your desire for trouble."

"The very end." Laney took both of Sandrine's hands. "This all feels like a strange dream."

"More like a nightmare, but now it is over. Or at least as soon as Theresa Aguilar goes to trial."

"Then what?"

"You will be a witness."

"No, I mean, and then what for us?"

Sandrine kissed her gently. "We begin again."

About the Author

Lisa Girolami has been in the entertainment industry since 1979. She holds a BA in Fine Art and an MS in Psychology. Previous jobs included ten years as a production executive in the motion picture industry and another two decades producing and designing theme parks for Disney and Universal Studios. She is now a Senior Producer/Director of Walt Disney Imagineering in Los Angeles and a counselor at a mental health facility in Garden Grove.

Writing has been a passion for her since she wrote and illustrated her first comic books at the restless age of six. Her imagination usually gets the best of her and plotting her next novel during boring corporate meetings keeps her from going stir-crazy. She currently lives with her partner, Susan, in Long Beach, California.

Lisa Girolami may be contacted via www.LisaGirolami.com.

Books Available From Bold Strokes Books

The Pleasure Set by Lisa Girolami. Laney DeGraff, a successful president of a family-owned bank on Rodeo Drive, finds her comfortable life taking a turn toward danger when Theresa Aguilar, a sleek, sexy lawyer, invites her to join an exclusive, secret group of powerful, alluring women. (978-1-60282-144-6)

A Perfect Match by Erin Dutton. The exciting world of pro golf forms the backdrop for a fast-paced, sexy romance. (978-1-60282-145-3)

Truths by Rebecca S. Buck. Two women separated by two hundred years are connected by fate and love. (978-1-60282-146-0)

Father Knows Best by Lynda Sandoval. High school juniors and best friends Lila Moreno, Meryl Morganstern, and Caressa Thibodoux plan to make the most of the summer before senior year. What they discover that amazing summer about girl power, growing up, and trusting friends and family more than prepares them to tackle that all-important senior year! (978-1-60282-147-7)

The Midnight Hunt by L.L. Raand. Medic Drake McKennan takes a chance and loses, and her life will never be the same—because when she wakes up after surviving a life-threatening illness, she is no longer human. (978-1-60282-140-8)

Long Shot by D. Jackson Leigh. Love isn't safe, which is exactly why equine veterinarian Tory Greyson wants no part of it—until Leah Montgomery and a horse that won't give up convince her otherwise. (978-1-60282-141-5)

In Medias Res by Yolanda Wallace. Sydney has forgotten her entire life, and the one woman who holds the key to her memory, and her heart, doesn't want to be found. (978-1-60282-142-2)

Awakening to Sunlight by Lindsey Stone. Neither Judith or Lizzy is looking for companionship, and certainly not love—but when their lives become entangled, they discover both. (978-1-60282-143-9)